THE CASTLE
AND
THE SCROLL

Book One in the Scroll Saga

This book is dedicated to my children and their offspring.

Always consult the Scroll.

The Castle and the Scroll

Copyright © 2018

Author: Jared Dodd

Editor: A'ndrea McAdams and many helpful readers

Cover and book design: Amy Dodd

Second Edition - Printed in the U.S.A.

Prelude

The two dragons made their way slowly through the thick forest. The younger one was fifteen feet in length, still small for a dragon. His companion was an elder dragon and was as large as a cottage. As they approached the edge of the forest, they crouched low as to conceal themselves.

"There," the older one said, pointing into the sunlit prairie.

The younger followed its elder's gaze to a large Castle, nestled atop a gentle rise in the hill.

"That's our enemy?" the novice asked, his voice reflecting his disgust.

"That's where they meet," the other said. "Look, they are exiting the Castle now."

Men, women, and children armed with swords, bows, and arrows began walking across the grassland, heading back to their homes.

"They look so weak," the younger said, his tongue shooting back and forth between his jagged teeth. "Why don't we gather together our clan and attack the Castle as they meet? Surely, oh wise one, an all-out offensive is our best chance of success."

"What a fool you are!" the elder dragon said with an anger that caused his accomplice to cower in fear. "You still have much to learn. We will not fight them head to head. We will fight them a different way."

"How?"

"From inside their own ranks," the elder said with a crafty smile on his face. "We will defeat them without them ever knowing."

1

"How will we do that?" the other said, amazed at the concept.

"It is simple," the elder said. "We will take the words of their king and twist them in such a way that they will think they are serving him, but in the end, they will only be serving themselves."

"How is this possible?" the younger dragon asked, smiling with wicked delight. "Won't they realize they are being deceived?"

"Not at all," said the elder. "Not until it's too late."

Chapter 1

You will likely believe, as you read my story, that you understand it on the outset. Let me warn you that it will not likely be, for I did not see the truth until the end, and even now, as I continue down the narrow path, the scales continue to fall. I grew up the only child of my parents, loved dearly by them, and content with my life. I had always known of Castles, since I was young, for almost every town or village had at least one, and some towns had many. When I was around the age of nine, I asked my father why there were Castles in every town. He replied that the followers of the Great King gathered there. I asked him who the Great King was, and he was silent. I knew what that meant; my father was only quiet on topics which displeased him. I asked my mother that evening, as she was tucking me into bed, about the Great King. She told me that He was the greatest of all warriors and that the Castles were where His armies trained.

"What do they train for?" I asked her.

"They train to kill dragons," she replied.

"You mean the dragons in the forests?" I asked with amazement. All of our people, and those of the neighboring villages, knew of the dragons. They lived in the forest and would never come out.

"Yes," my mother said softly, brushing her fingers through my hair.

"But how?" I asked puzzled. "I thought the dragons were invincible."

"They are," she replied. "The Great King is nothing more than a fable, my son. No one is able to kill the dragons." As she said this, I could see pain in her eyes—a hurt that seemed to go back far into her memory.

"What's wrong, Mother? Why do you look so sad?"

"It's nothing," she replied. "I was just thinking of your grandparents. I wish you could have met them."

"Why were you thinking about them?" I asked her.

"They were followers of the Great King. And often, as a little girl, I would go with them to the Castle."

"What was it like?" I asked with a big yawn, fighting hard against the heaviness of my eyes so I could hear the story.

"Well," she said, "it was big and extravagant. And there were many nice people there. But in the end, it was all pretend."

I was certain my mother could read my expression. She knew I wanted an explanation, for I was questioning her with my eyes.

"I know this is hard for you to understand," she said slowly and quietly. "But the Castle promised your grandparents that they would be able to kill dragons. Your grandparents believed them. And after much training, they went into the forest on a dragon hunt and never returned. I was still very young, just as you are now. And that's how I became an orphan. I was all on my own, until I met your father. It was a hard and difficult childhood. What kind of *Great King* would do something like that?"

My mother didn't answer any more of my questions that evening, for she said that the Great King was just a bedtime story and not true. And even though I wanted to believe her, there was still something in the idea of the Great King that touched the depths of my heart. From that day forward, when I passed the Castle near our home on King's Day, I would enjoy looking at all the men, women, and children, entering with their bows, swords, and shields.

My best friend, Lily, lived close by. She was a year younger than me. She knew some things concerning the legend of the Great King, and we would often pretend together, I with my sword and she with her bow. We had a motto that we came up with: *Down with the Dragon and all his race!* Lily was beautiful. I often dreamt of us growing up and fighting dragons together as we followed the Great King.

One day we challenged each other to go into the forest. We knew we weren't allowed to, but our imaginations got the best of us. We had convinced ourselves that we were both warriors of the Great King who could defeat any dragon. We slowly crept into the forest and began to dare each other to go deeper.

"You're barely in," Lily said to me. She was a good fifteen yards further along. "Don't be afraid, Caleb; we are warriors of the Great King, remember?"

I cautiously advanced and was soon slightly past Lily. I was just about to dare her to go further when I heard something. It was a voice—the voice of a woman.

"My dears, how brave you are. What precious and powerful children you must be to come within the forest."

Neither of us could see the woman, but we could both hear her, and her voice was coming from deeper within the forest. We slowly made our way together, hand in hand.

"Keep coming," she said gently and smoothly. "Such brave warriors must be honored. A great feast awaits, with all the goodies and treats that a hungry warrior needs."

Lily made me stop. "Wait," she said. "It's a trap."

"But it's just a woman," I said, and though I didn't want to admit it, I was charmed by the woman's voice.

We continued to advance, and still we heard her. And though I could not see the woman, I could picture her. I saw her as tall and elegant, with long dark hair. Her skin was fair and without blemish. All within me now wanted to see her. It didn't matter what the consequence would be.

"Surely you won't stop now," the woman said, sounding only a small distance away.

"Who are you?" I asked. Lily's grip on my hand tightened.

"Who am I?" repeated the woman. "I am your friend. Your very best friend in the whole wide world. Come with me and I will show you wonderful things. Come just a little bit closer. I've been waiting for you two. I've heard of you. I can't wait to bring you deeper into the forest."

Lily whispered only loud enough for me to hear it. "Caleb, I'm scared."

I cared about Lily's safety, but my captivation of this unseen woman was the stronger emotion. Then, suddenly, I heard footsteps approaching from behind us, crunching the drying leaves of autumn with every step. Was it my parents, or friends of the woman, or someone else? There was a large oak tree only a few feet away with a hollowed trunk. Pulling Lily with me, I quickly dashed within the tree, which seemed to shield us from both the woman and the steps that were approaching.

Voices now accompanied the footsteps, and they were the voices of two men. The men continued to advance until they were right next to us, though they didn't see us. I then heard the woman's voice.

"Stop," she said.

The two men were startled but quickly regained their composure.

"Who are you two and why have you come here?" she said, her voice sounding agitated.

"We are hunters," the men replied. "We came to scout out this area for game."

"Don't you worry about the dragons?" the woman asked.

"The dragons are growing scarcer in these parts," one man said. "Where are you? Show yourself."

"All in good time," the woman replied, and I found myself frustrated that these two men had interfered with my conversation with her.

"I was visiting with two young people," the woman said. "One of them was very special to me. That child, I was very excited to meet. But it seems you have frightened them off."

"What are you talking about?" asked the other hunter. "No children ever enter the forest."

The woman breathed so loudly I could hear her. It was as if she was only a small stone's throw away. "Never mind," she said at last. "Why don't you two men follow me? I will show you things better than mere game. Come. Are you hungry? Food eaten in secret is delicious. Come taste the wine I have mixed. It will delight your souls."

I then heard the footsteps of the men continue. Peering around the tree trunk, I saw the two hunters walking deeper within the forest. Lily was relieved. I, however, was appalled.

"We must go after them," I said.

"Have you lost your mind?" Lily asked. "We must leave!"

"Hurry," I said, trying to force Lily to come with me. "We must see her."

"No, Caleb," she replied. "We must leave now."

I then began to climb up the tree within which we had been hiding. Lily, out of either fear or allegiance, followed me.

"What are you doing?" she asked with frustration.

"I must see her," I replied. "Just one quick glance."

We were about twenty feet up, and I could scarcely see the men through the thicket of the forest."

"No more playing games," one of them said. "Where are you?"

"I am here," the woman said.

I then saw a very large, black dragon pick up both men off of the ground, one in each claw. The dragon spoke, and it had the woman's voice.

"What fools you are," the dragon said. And as it spoke its voice changed from feminine to masculine.

The men shouted out in horror. My last sight, before jumping to the ground and running away with Lily beside me, was the dragon shoving both men into its mouth and devouring them whole.

Chapter 2

We turned away from the tree and began to run toward the edge of the forest. No sound was heard behind us; the silence was more frightening than the earlier sounds of carnage.

We ran all the way to our homes without stopping. For a long time, we didn't speak, for we were both suffering from shock.

"Let's never go to the forest again," Lily said at last.

"I agree," I said. "I don't understand. That voice, who was that?"

"That was the dragon," said Lily. "My father told me they will sometimes speak. They do it to lure people into the forest."

"Why didn't you ever tell me?" I asked.

"I didn't think it was true," she said. "Besides, I tried to tell you, but you didn't listen. What was wrong with you?"

I thought back to the feelings I had when I heard the voice. "I don't know how to describe it," I said. "It was as if I was under some kind of charm or evil magic. I couldn't resist."

9

"You must believe," Lily said. "Only true believers of the Great King can resist the dragons' deceitfulness. They are liars."

"Does that mean I don't believe?" I asked, filled with sincere concern for my soul. "Does that mean I'm not in His army?"

"I don't know," Lily said, her eyes full of tears. "But those men are dead. That could have been us, Caleb. That image will haunt me forever."

"That dragon was black," I said in continued shock. "I thought that dragons were only red."

"Me too," Lily said, trying to speak amongst her tears. "I've never heard of a black dragon. You don't suppose it was *the* Dragon, do you?"

"No," I replied. "But whatever it was, it said that one of us was special." I tried to hold back my tears. "You don't think it will come after us, do you?"

"It can't," Lily said. "Dragons never leave the forest. But still, what if it lures us again, or does the same to one of our neighbors or friends?"

I felt a conviction rise from deep within me. Even at such a young age I knew that something must be done.

"We must get help," I said. "We can't fight for the Great King on our own. We need to be trained."

"How?" asked Lily.

"We need to go to a Castle," I replied.

"But your parents won't let you go to a Castle," Lily said. "And my family only goes to the Castle twice a year, during the festivals."

"We must try to find a way," I pleaded.

"But Caleb," she said, "maybe your parents are correct; maybe it's impossible to kill dragons. I don't see how in the world we could have killed that dragon today. They are invincible."

I didn't know what to think. My mind was filled with all kinds of emotion, mainly doubt. I kept trying to erase from my mind the final image I saw of those two men and their last moment on this earth.

"I don't want to not believe," I said after some time. "I want the Great King to be real. The thought of Him being only a fairytale breaks my heart. It makes me feel empty."

Lily was still crying. "I want Him to be real too," she said. "I'm just afraid. The dragons scare me."

"Don't be afraid, Lily," I said. "I will learn how to fight dragons, and I will protect you."

"How?"

"I'm going to go to the Castle. Tomorrow is King's Day, and all of the soldiers of the Great King will be assembling. And I will be there."

"The sun is setting," Lily said. "I must go home."

"Are you going to be alright?" I asked.

"Yes. I just need to get some sleep," she said. "I will see you tomorrow?"

"Of course," I said, my heart drawn back to this young girl who was my dearest friend. "I will come and get you. And together, we will go to the Castle of the Great King."

I turned to go home, and then I heard Lily's voice.

"Caleb?" she said.

I turned to her.

"Down with the Dragon and all his race," she said, trying to force a smile.

"Down with the Dragon and all his race," I repeated.

That evening, as I lay in bed, my mind was racing. The events of that day seemed like a dream, though I knew they were real. I had heard the rumbling of dragons before, and had spoken to those who had seen them, but I had never had an encounter with a dragon. And this dragon was black, as black as night. What did that mean? Despite my doubts and questions, my heart was resolute. I would learn how to fight dragons. I would follow the Great King. I would be able to protect Lily, and I would never be deceived by a dragon again. I meditated on how the dragon had said that it was excited to meet one of us. I wondered what that meant. Did it know who I was? Did it know that my grandparents were dragon fighters? A shiver ran up my spine.

As I began to drift to sleep, a dream quickly came to me. I dreamt that a giant, black dragon was walking throughout my village, searching for me. I could hear it, stepping and slithering through the alleys. *But dragons never exit the forest*, I thought to myself. And yet the dream continued. It was peering in window after window, its yellow eyes piercing into the darkness, looking for its prey. Every home was one less home to search. Soon, it would come to its desired location. I then dreamt that in frustration, the beast began to set homes ablaze. Smoke, sulfur, and fire poured from its mouth. The dream was so real. I could feel the heat of the flames and could smell the smoke. It was getting hotter. My skin began to sweat. My lungs began to burn.

Suddenly I awoke, coughing and confused. I wasn't sure how much of my dream was true, but one thing was certain. The fire was real. My entire room was quickly being overcome with flames!

Chapter 3

I could scarcely see anything amidst the heat and smoke. I felt I would pass out at any moment and quickly fell upon the floor, reaching over, with eyes closed, to where I thought the window was. I sprang upon the window with such force that the shudders burst open and I tumbled outside to the ground. The flames were all around me, and at that moment I observed that the fire wasn't restricted to my house alone. It seemed like the entire village was consumed.

"Run boy!" said a robed figure not too far away. Everything was in chaos. People were everywhere. The flames and smoke were all across the landscape. I felt that I was going to burst into flames myself, for the heat was unbearable. Only one thing was on my mind: Lily.

I immediately tried to run to her house, but it was difficult because the heat was so unforgiving. I got to where I could see her home; it was engulfed and fully ablaze. The same robed figure I saw before now took hold of me.

"Run away from the fire!" he commanded. "It will soon kill us all! Run!" I ran toward the pastures which were, fortunately, close to my home. I called out for my parents; no answer. The next few hours were filled with screams and pandemonium which set in my mind like a fogged nightmare. Soon the sun was rising, and most of the fires had finished their work, still smoldering in the rubble. Half of our village was left in ruins. All of the village had assembled in the village square, except for those still helping recover victims and finish off the flames. I searched and searched for both Lily and my parents, but to no avail.

"Lily!" I shouted. "Lily! Mother! Father!"

It was light enough now to move about safely. I quickly ran back to my home. Nothing left but ashes. I then went to Lily's home. It was also gone. I called out again for her, but no answer.

"She's gone," said a voice. It was a kind lady who lived close by, who I only knew by sight. "I heard her screams only a few seconds before the structure collapsed. She and her parents are gone. I fear that your parents were also taken. But praise the fates that you are safe."

I refused to accept the woman's words. I ran to the other side of Lily's house for some sign of her escape. And there I was faced with the hard truth. Three corpses, the likes of which I will not try to describe, were left within the destruction. They were charred and horrid and were clearly the remains of two adults and a child. I fell to my knees, weeping. In the same day, I had lost my parents and my soul mate; my three closest friends. I was now an orphan, just as my mother had been. And Lily, the girl who had captured my heart, was dead.

I had no one. No next of kin. No friends. Someone might take me in, out of pity. But I didn't want it. At that fateful moment, something happened inside of me. There were two things that I was certain of, which that day were seared upon my mind. First, I was on my own. And second, that the Great King was only a fairytale. My mother was right. There was no Great King. There was no such thing as killing dragons. Never again would I say, *Down with the Dragon and all his race*. That part of me was dead. A darkness entered my heart, and a new emotion which I had never known became real to me: the emotion of bitterness.

There, only a few feet away from Lily's home, were our toy weapons still unscathed upon the ground. I picked up my sword and her bow and threw them within the ashes which still fumed.

"You have anyone?" the woman asked.

"No," I replied, my eyes free from tears, my soul free from emotion.

"You can stay with me, if you'd like," she said kindly, "for a time, until we can find you another home."

"No," I said. "I can't stay here. I'm going far away. Farewell."

I walked to the west, never looking back.

For many years I roamed from village to village, living off the mercy of others. I always avoided the Castles in every village. A part of my heart hated them, yet another part of me, deep down, was still drawn to them. At the age of fifteen, I found steady work at a blacksmith shop in the village of Greystone. The owner, a kind man named William, hired me as his apprentice. He was a childless widower, and I became a son to him. He taught me everything he knew about blacksmithing. For the first time in years, I had a home and something resembling a parent. My hope and joy regarding life began to return, slowly.

My life was simple and reserved. I worked most of the day and stayed mainly to myself. My only friends were William and the occasional visit of a young man named Justin. I met Justin only a few weeks after coming into the service of William. He was from my home village of Ravenhill.

"I am also from Ravenhill," I said, a part of me fascinated at seeing one of my own people.

"How did you end up here in Greystone?" he asked kindly.

"I left after the Great Fire."

"That was a terrible time for our people," he said solemnly. "It took our village many months to recover, though now, by the grace of the Great King, we are prosperous again."

When Justin mentioned the Great King, a pit entered my stomach. I guessed that he noticed the slight reaction upon my face.

"Justin comes here every eight weeks or so with crops for some of our people," William explained. "We barter with him some of our own goods."

Justin and William then entered into negotiations which seemed very familiar for both of them. Justin had potatoes, onions, carrots, and kale. William traded him wheel bearings, nails, and horseshoes.

"It was nice to meet you, Caleb," Justin said. "It's always nice to meet a fellow citizen of Ravenhill."

"Likewise," I replied, trying to be civil. "But that place is no longer my home. All that I loved was reduced to ashes on that day."

"I am sorry," he replied. "But be assured, that even though the Great King's ways don't always make sense to us, they are always part of His ultimate plan."

I had no reply for such words, and so I simply nodded my head as a sign of respect. Justin packed up his wagon and headed back to Ravenhill. William spoke concerning Justin as he rode over the plains.

"He's a good man," he said. "He brings good trade to this village, and he is extremely generous to the widow and her five children across the way. He is obviously an ardent follower of the Great King. I myself have never seen a need for the Castle, but I do respect Justin for his character."

"With all due respect to Justin," I replied, "he is fooled. The Great King is not real."

"You may be correct," William answered. "But with the dragons multiplying, and their influence upon mankind, one can only hope that He is real."

"Influence?" I asked. "*Supposed influence* sounds better. It's never been proven that they influence anyone."

"It has to me," William said. "Whenever the dragons get closer to the edge of the forest, something seems to happen to the hearts of people. You cannot deny,

Caleb, that there is such a thing as good and evil. The dragons, they are the epitome of evil. My question is: who then is the epitome of good?'"

I had no answer to give.

Four years passed quickly in Greystone. I continued to grow in my knowledge of blacksmithing and enjoyed working with William. I did, bit by bit, get out more into the society of Greystone. The people there were kind. I was coming to the age when young men start thinking of marriage. William encouraged me in this end, but I felt hardened to it, for I knew that my true love had left the planet many years earlier. I did hope to one day find another, but the thought still brought pain to my heart.

One evening, while William and I were closing up the shop, he encouraged me. "Caleb, you don't want to end up all alone like me. My wife died many years ago, and we never had children. Now look at me. I have you, for which I am thankful, but that was luck. Find yourself a good woman. You know the trade of blacksmithing now to a point where you could easily provide for a family."

"You might be right, William," I said, "but for me, such a woman would have to be something pretty special."

"You're being selfish," William said. "You're protecting your heart against pain, to the point where you're going to push good people away. You have to trust that there's a greater plan out there for you."

"Ha," I replied. "You're beginning to sound like Justin."

"And what's wrong with that?" asked William. "Justin is a man unafraid of the future. He has a real and true hope. He sees that there is someone in control of all of this. What if he's right? What if, even though things seem crazy to us, that there really is someone in control? What if this is all part of His plan, part of His story?"

"His plan?" I asked sarcastically. "You mean the plan of a warrior from centuries ago that rode off into the sunset, leaving us to fight His battles on our own? I don't know, William."

"Well," he said humbly, "I suppose that one day we will all know the truth. I hope though that we turn out on the right side. We only have one life after all. There is no rough draft. We have one life, pressed over the forming fires of this world, to be shaped into a certain kind of person. I hope we end up being a tool or weapon useful to our Maker."

I had no reply.

"Get yourself to bed, Caleb. I will finish up here."

I did as I was told and was soon lying in my bed. As I lay there, I wondered about William's words. Was there someone in control of life and its circumstances? Or, was everything chaos and chance? It was obvious to me that the world was full of order. Olive seeds made olive trees, and when the shepherdess bred her flock, she ended up with sheep. The stars were always in the same place, and the sun and moon followed their cycles. There was much order but also much chaos. Order in what had been made, but chaos in the lives of people. As I was thinking through these things, I began to hear raised voices in the distance. *Likely a celebration of some kind,* I thought. But then I noticed that the cries were filled with fear and seemed to be multiplying. Something was happening. I got out of bed and looked out of my window. What I beheld shocked me. There were some women and men running across the moonlit prairie with others chasing behind them. The pursuers were carrying axes and swords. I watched with horror as an axe was thrown, lodging itself into the back of a villager. I then heard William's voice from the other side of the cottage.

"Raiders!" he shouted. "Caleb, quick! Run away! Raiders are here!"

Chapter 4

I quickly sprang from my room and hurried into the workshop. William was gone, and the door wide open. I didn't know what to do. Upon the table was a large hammer. Without much thought, I grabbed it and ran out into the evening air. People were running everywhere. I immediately recognized the raiders, for their appearance matched the description I had always heard of them. They were raiders of the north; evil men who, instead of working for their daily bread, made their living by plundering good, honest people. I found William; he was taking his stand with some other men of our village. Many men of the north had surrounded them, armed with swords and axes. A few of the villagers were armed with real weapons, though many had spades and pitchforks. I quickly ran toward them, and hitting an unsuspecting raider on the head, I came beside my fellow citizens.

"Foolish lad!" William yelled amidst the carnage. "I told you to run!"

Cries and mayhem were everywhere, and fires were beginning to spread. I stood my ground next to William and the others as we fought off the raiders. The man across from me thrust his spear at me. I grabbed it and came down upon him with my hammer. The blow seemed to shock the raiders, and they quickly ran in different directions. William and I caught our breaths and ran to the aid of others.

Dead bodies were everywhere. Not far away, two raiders were attempting to break in the front door of the home of Joanna, the widow who Justin often assisted in the feeding of her family. I could hear the cries of Joanna and her five children from within the cottage.

"Come!" William said to me, and we ran to their aid.

The two raiders saw us coming and prepared for the encounter. William was a very large man, and simply threw himself into one of the men, knocking him upon the outer wall of the house. The other came at me with a spear. I dodged the first blow and was able to strike the man upon his side, knocking him down. I then looked back toward William. His opponent had now regained his footing and was violently swinging his sword upon William's staff. I struck the man upon his head, sending him to the ground, never to rise again. William got up with an expression of gratitude on his face. Horror quickly returned and he moved me out of the way of an oncoming blow from my first assailant. The spear thrust, which was intended for me, sank deep within William's belly. I cried out in anger and finished off the raider. I fell to my knees next to William, weeping with bitter rage and anger.

"Don't cry," William said, trying to hide his level of pain. "This is all as it should be."

I quickly looked around. The streets were clearing now and the danger was dissipating.

"You are the only family I have," I said, eyes full of tears. "I can't go on without you."

"Nonsense," he said. "You have fought well. You have saved the life of the family in this home. You are a man now. You must stop running from the darkness that haunts you. Your destiny is only found on the other side of facing your past."

"You believe in destiny now?" I asked with as much a smile as I could produce.

"I do," William replied, his eyes starting to look beyond this life to the one that follows. "I believe in Him, Caleb. I believe in the Great King. I wish I could go back, and do life different now, but I can't. But for you, my son, your life is before you. Don't end up all alone and without purpose like me. Find the truth and follow it."

William died in my arms, and for nearly an hour I held him and wept. Joanna and her children soon came out and wept with me. By the time the sun began to rise, all the dead bodies had been gathered at the village cemetery, nearly sixty souls. The bodies of dead raiders were burnt in a pile outside of town. By noon, all sixty of the dead of Greystone were buried. I stood at the foot of William's tomb. I was reminded of standing before my parents' home, nothing remaining of the life I knew. And here I was again. I held on to William's dying words. *Find the truth and follow it.* They were both a source of life and death to me, a source of strength and bitterness. I felt a hand upon my shoulder. It was Justin.

"I just arrived half an hour ago," he said. "I am struck with heartache and grief. I'm so sorry."

I remained silent, my thoughts still rolling over themselves in my mind.

"He was a good man," Justin continued. "And he loved you as a son."

"So," I spoke slowly, "was this part of His plan? Was this the doing of the Great King?"

"That is a difficult question to answer," Justin said. "In such moments as these, it is hard to imagine anything such as this to be the will of the Great King. But in the end, though it doesn't always make sense to us, the Great King is working everything out for His glorious end."

"It will please you to know that William died believing in the Great King," I said.

"That does indeed warm my heart," Justin replied. "I always sensed that William knew, deep down, that the Great King was true."

"His final actions proved it," I testified, "for he died saving my life, at the peril of his own."

"Not only did he save your life," Justin said, "but together, the two of you saved the lives of Joanna and her children. I am forever grateful for your service to them. According to the Scroll, William died with honor. It was a glorious death."

"Yes," I agreed. "I suppose it was."

"William believed in you, Caleb. And he has left you a good life here. His home and shop and tools are all here, for you. You can live on in peace and security."

"It would seem so," I said plainly. "But I think not."

"What do you mean?" Justin asked, his voice filled with concern.

I turned and looked him in the eyes.

"Did you bring your wagon?" I asked.

"Of course," he answered. "I plan to give all of my produce to the village as a gift, seeing what has happened here. Then I will quickly return home."

"Good," I answered. "Do you have room for one more?"

Chapter 5

Justin went to the home of Joanna and gifted her half of his produce; the rest he gave to the Castle of Greystone. Fortunately, this left his wagon empty, leaving plenty of room for me to load up all of the blacksmithing tools that I would need to make a living elsewhere. Although my heart continued to grieve for William, I knew that what I was doing would please him. By midafternoon, Justin and I were on our way. Justin informed me that we wouldn't reach the borders of Ravenhill until late into the night.

"Despite your loss," Justin said, "I am pleased that you've been so well provided for. These tools are worth many months' wages. Ravenhill is lacking young and skilled blacksmiths. You should do very well there."

"I hope so," I said soberly. "I hope for a life with some kind of meaning."

"Well," replied Justin, jumping at the opportunity, "if you want meaning, you should follow the Great King."

"But the Great King is a fairytale," I said respectfully. "No one has ever seen Him. Dragons continue to roam the forest at will. I see your people, exiting the Castle every King's Day, but I don't see them killing dragons."

23

Justin smiled. "Things aren't always what they seem," he said. "We do kill dragons. You don't see it because you don't join us. Just last autumn, we killed a large dragon. Besides," he continued, "the Castle isn't just about killing dragons."

"I'm listening," I said sincerely.

"It's about being a family, about being devoted to each other. I've gotten to know you well, Caleb. You were an orphan. Now you're alone again. You have no one. Why not come be a part of something big and real? The Great King desires to be a father to all of us. All we must do is follow Him. William, in his last hour, believed in the Great King. Do you think him a fool?"

There's no way I could call William a fool. I loved him too much, and if I was honest with myself, I believed that William was right. I did, deep down, believe that the Great King was real. But there was another issue.

"Alright," I said. "Let's say that the Great King is real. Is He good? I mean, what if His ways aren't good? Every person dear to me has died before my eyes. Is that the doing of one who is good?"

"This is what I've tried to tell you in the past," Justin said respectfully. "And yet my words won't be enough. The lights, within your soul must ignite. The Great King is just and good and true in all He does. Yet, this is the hard part for us to understand, His ways are not our ways. His ways will often seem unfair, or wrong, but that is only because He is able to see the end from the beginning. Who am I, Caleb, or who are you, to question the Great King? He has been from the beginning. We are young. And yet, He allows us to join His army and be with Him."

I was able to intellectually understand the words which Justin spoke. I could understand them, but I didn't like them. I didn't want to confess or agree with the idea that all of my life thus far was a *good plan*. And yet the dying words of William echoed in my heart. I had to face my nightmares. And the only way to do that, I was beginning to see, was to join with Justin and the Castle. If the Great King was real, and if He was good, then the only path to answering my questions was to follow Him. In order to understand the One I criticized, I had to love Him.

"And what does He require?" I asked. "To be part of His army, what does it cost me?"

"You must meet together with us, every King's Day. You must learn about Him and His Kingdom. You must train to kill dragons."

Justin could see the hesitation on my face. He could tell that I was counting the cost. He continued to pursue me. "Don't you want to grip the sword and the bow? Don't you want to have a shield of your own? We are all part of the story of good against evil. Long ago the Great King and the Great Dragon began a war that still rages today. Don't you want to fulfill your destiny by fighting for the Great King?"

As Justin spoke, my heart was touched with feelings from my childhood, feelings that I had buried years before. The desire of being part of a real family, devoted to each other, and devoted to the Great King was something I couldn't deny. I wanted it, more and more, with all of my heart. It was as if Lily was cheering me on, from some faraway place in the sky. It was as if she was telling me that I could trust the Great King. I sat quietly, for over an hour upon that wagon thinking and feeling; more and more my heart was settled. I wanted to be a warrior for the Great King.

"Very well then," I said at last. "How many days is it until King's Day?"

Chapter 6

Justin allowed me to spend the night at his farmhouse. Early the next morning we went to the sight of my old home. The plot was still empty, used by a neighbor as a place for her sheep to graze. It was sobering to look upon that place, as well as Lily's home site, which was likewise empty. The neighbors were overjoyed to see me and agreed to let me build on my family's land immediately. I would make a simple home, with a blacksmith shop attached, and would sell my goods in the market in the mornings. Justin said he and others from the Castle would help me. We began to lay the bottom logs down the next morning. Fortunately, with the money I received from William's death, in addition to my own savings, it would only take about a week to get my home built.

Justin also introduced me to Simon, the local constable. He would be an important man to know since I was a laborer, and he the tax collector. Justin made the situation very clear to me.

"Pay your taxes on time," he said, "and you won't have anything to worry about regarding Simon."

The first day I arrived back in Ravenhill was a Tuesday, and I eagerly awaited King's Day. That week I and others from the Castle, along with hired laborers, worked on the blacksmithing cottage. I thought I saw, from time to time, a hooded figure from within the forest, not too far away, peering out from within the brush. He was far away, but I could tell he had a long, white beard. I couldn't help but feel that he was looking at me, and I wondered what kind of fool would set foot within the forest.

By Saturday my home and blacksmith shop were finished, with the exception of a few minor additions which I could do as needed. I was eager to begin my work in Ravenhill, and I was also eager to start my training in the army of the Great King.

The next day was King's Day, and I went to the Castle for the very first time. It was extremely intimidating, but Justin promised he would stay by my side and explain everything. As we approached the Castle, I was able to see up close the weaponry I had always admired as a child. There were swords, shield, bows, and arrows. As we entered the Castle, I could feel the love and acceptance that seemed to radiate from within. People greeted me with the handshake of true brotherhood and friendship. It was as if a family reunion was happening, and everyone loved each other. Conversations, smiles, and laughter filled the air. We then made our way into the Great Hall of the Castle. There we all stood together, with the rays of the sun shining through the windows, and someone began a hymn of praise to the Great King. All present pledged their undying love and allegiance to the Great King through song. Afterwards, we were all seated, and a man got up on the platform in the front of the Great Hall. He was clad in full armor and his sword was like nothing I had ever seen before. When he spoke, his voice boomed like a cannon.

"Who is that man?" I asked Justin.

"He is our captain," he replied. "Captain David. Every Castle has a captain. They are the greatest of all our warriors, and they often travel in the forest and kill dragons."

I was awestruck. All of those childhood years, just down the road from my home, was a group of warriors, fighting for the Great King. But never had I known that they had a captain!

"Let us pledge our allegiance to the Great King!" he shouted.

Everyone then repeated these words: "We live for the Great King. We die for the Great King. The Dragon, and his children, will not avail. We will train. We will fight. We will have the victory."

Another hymn of praise began. There were flutes and violins accompanying our voices. I felt like I was in a dream. I had no doubt left in my heart: this was the greatest opportunity given to mankind. My bitterness was lifted, and true love was put in its place. I was a follower of the Great King. My life would never be the same again.

Then I saw the captain unroll a Scroll and read from it. The words from that Scroll cannot be adequately described in the space of this narrative. Suffice it to say, they were words like no mere man could form. Every word pierced my heart with the sharpness of an arrow but with the gentleness of a father's embrace. I asked Justin about the Scroll.

"They are the words of the Great King," he said enthusiastically. "He gave them to us so we would know how to train for fighting the dragons, and so that we would never be led astray."

A letter straight from the Great King, I thought. It seemed too good to be true. Captain David then spoke of the Scroll and what it said. We all sat and listened, and afterward sang a hymn of warfare. Then the captain asked if there were any who had chosen, for the first time, to serve the Great King. All was still. Justin looked over at me.

"You should go up to the front," he said.

"I will if you come with me," I replied.

We went together, and I met Captain David and told him about my choice to serve the Great King. He brought me upon the platform and presented me to the gathering. They all cheered. Two other men then came upon the stage bearing a sword and a bow. They handed them to Captain David and he presented them to me.

"This day you have become a warrior of the Great King," he said aloud for all to hear. "We will teach you the ways of the sword and the bow. You will kill dragons."

The entire congregation erupted in shouts of joy and victory. Captain David had me remain in the front of the Great Hall, where nearly everyone in the Castle greeted me and encouraged me. I left the Castle that day with a transformed sense of purpose and destiny. I couldn't stop thinking about the Great King. I was also fixed upon Captain David, for he seemed to me to be the greatest warrior I had ever met, and I longed to be like him. I asked Justin how people become captains.

"There are Great Castles," he explained, "far from here. Certain men and women go there, and after much training, they become captains."

I wondered if I would ever go to a Great Castle. At the time, it seemed like a far-off dream.

I returned to my home that day excited and filled with joy. I knew my life would never be the same again. For the first time, I had to acknowledge that Justin's words were likely true; the plan of the Great King was best.

During the following week, all I could think about was going back to the Castle. I honestly wondered how everyone was content with only meeting once a week. I would have loved to meet and learn and worship together every day. Fortunately, I had Justin to answer questions for me.

That next King's Day I returned to the Castle, and the experience was the same. It was wonderful and I didn't want to leave. I continued to meet more people, all of whom were very kind and in love with the Great King. I stayed until they began to close and lock the doors. I was able to visit some more with Captain David and then walked home with an attitude of joy. I thought back to the fact that only a few weeks earlier, I was in the village of Greystone, hardhearted and bitter towards the Castle. Now I never wanted to miss a meeting. I was just about at my house when I heard a voice behind me. It was Justin.

"Caleb!" he shouted. "Hurry! Captain David has called for you!"

Chapter 7

"Me?" I asked with surprise.

"Yes," answered Justin excitedly. "There is an urgent need concerning a potential army recruit, and Captain David is putting together a small team and wanted you to be on it. You must come right away!"

Together we jogged to a small cottage by the river where Captain David and eight other men were already gathered.

"Ah," Captain David said, as he noticed us, "now we are all here."

I then noticed a woman with two small children standing nearby. It appeared that she was a single mother and quite poor. She had two young daughters, around two and four years of age.

Captain David put his arm around the woman. "Let me introduce you all to Mary. She is a kind woman, but she is all alone. Her husband fled nearly a year ago now and left the burden of parent and provider on sweet Mary. We are here to make repairs to her home, encourage her, and love on her children."

Mary smiled slightly with gratitude, though I could tell she was ashamed. The men and I worked on the house, spoke with Mary, and played with the children.

This went on all throughout the afternoon and into the early evening. Captain David had brought supplies and tools, and so we were able to repair her roof, some breaks in the walls, and other simple house issues. We also took turns playing with the girls. They were sweet and innocent, and my heart hurt for them that they had to be raised without a father. I was able to attain more of Mary's story; her husband was a man of ruined reputation. No one had heard from him since the day he left the village. Mary worked washing clothes in the river for other families and barely made enough for her family to live on. I overheard Captain David talking to her.

"We will try to help as we can," he was saying. "I hope that you will consider coming to the Castle every King's Day. Your daughters need guidance and the Castle can offer it to you."

Mary was extremely grateful for the services given to her and her family. We all said farewell to the sweet sisters and I thought the younger began to cry as we left. My heart was touched, and I appreciated the Castle all the more. If only I had been connected to the Castle when my parents died. It would have saved me much trouble and pain.

As we walked back to the center of the village, I visited with the other men with whom I had been working. One of them was unfamiliar to me, that is, I had never seen him before. I knew that his name was Paul, for I had heard the other men speak to him during our service that afternoon.

"Paul," I said to him, "I haven't seen you at the Castle. Have you been away on business?"

"Not at all," Paul said cheerfully. "It's autumn and so it's marble season. My younglings have had tournaments the last three King's Days. I was fortunate to have been able to make this service mission."

"Marble season?" I asked curiously.

"Of course," he said. "You know how to play marbles, don't you?"

"Well, yes," I answered. "Though I've only played a few times."

"My son is on the village youngling marble team," Paul explained.

"And they play these tournaments on King's Day?" I asked a bit surprised.

"Yes, they do," Paul said with a voice of frustration at the situation. "They started doing that a few years back. My family, and many others from the Castle, disapproved. But in the end, what could we do?"

"Isn't it hard to miss the Castle?" I asked. My shock caused me to lose my tactfulness.

"Well, of course," Paul said, seeming a bit agitated at my question. "We are soldiers of the Great King, so it's obviously very hard to miss the Castle meetings. But what are we supposed to do? We want our younglings to develop well, and marbles is a special part of that. Just as checkers is in the spring."

"Checkers in the spring?" I said, not able to refrain from my surprise.

"You will have to forgive Caleb," Justin said chiming in. "He had a different upbringing then most and isn't accustomed to our commitment to games."

Paul nodded in kind understanding.

"I have actually found that the games are a great way to increase your faith in the Great King," said Aaron, another man who was there with us. "My son Jason always prays before his marble matches. He had his favorite verse of the Scroll stitched on his marble carrier."

"What verse is that?" I asked, curious at the conversation.

"It is from the book of weaponry," Aaron answered. "It reads, *The Great King trains my hands for war.*"

"That is a good one," Paul said. "My son has a verse on his marble carrier as well. It reads, *I can win all battles by the power of the Great King.*"

I was quite taken aback by what I was hearing. These men were quoting verses from the Scroll about warfare, battles, and the Great King, and they were applying it to marbles. Justin remained calm and unmoved as we walked along, so I figured that my concern was misplaced. Unfortunately, however, my tongue wasn't able to hold back my thinking.

"There's obviously nothing wrong with games," I began. "But don't you think you're confusing your children? When you miss the meeting of the Great King for a game tournament, what does that teach them?"

"Oh please," Paul said, seemingly upset. "No offense, but you're barely out of being a youngling yourself. Captain David encourages us in our games. You don't disagree with him, do you?"

I remained quiet.

Shortly after, we came to the town square, and most of the men parted ways while Justin and I continued on together.

"You don't want to come across judgmental," Justin said. "We have to respect the convictions and commitments of others."

"Forgive me," I said. "I know I'm still young, but I seriously don't understand. I'm confused."

"Let me help you," Justin said sincerely, as was his way. "What don't you understand?"

"We are soldiers of the Great King, training together to fight dragons and win the battle, right?"

"Absolutely," Justin agreed.

"And we are commanded to meet together in the Castle and train, correct?"

"Right again."

"Why then would a parent keep himself and his children away from the Castle for something as silly and worldly as marbles?" I asked.

"Careful what you say," Justin said looking around us. "Marbles and checkers aren't silly. There's actually a lot to learn from them. Teamwork, leadership, and perseverance to name a few. You should come out to the local matches if you're able. You'd be surprised how much fun they are. Paul's son is quite talented. One could even say that the Great King gave him the skill of marbles so he could bring glory to the Great King through the game."

Justin continued to ramble on. For the most part I tuned him out, concluding that marbles and checkers must be much more interesting and important than I had ever considered. Justin and I parted ways, and my thoughts turned to the day's events with Mary. Here was a woman who had no one and was on her own. But the Castle came to her rescue. This was the kind of life I wanted to live. I was now part of something big, something that could make a real difference in people's lives. Mary would hopefully be joining the Castle soon, and her children would experience the quality of life that only the Castle could bring.

As I approached my home, I noticed a small box on the ground in front of my front door. I picked it up and deciphered my name written upon it. Looking around cautiously, I opened the box. Almost immediately I recognized what was inside.

"It can't be," I said to myself.

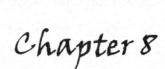

Chapter 8

It was a scroll. Somehow, even though I had never held one, or looked within it, I knew it was a copy of the Scroll of the Great King. I had planned on saving up for one, for they were extremely expensive, but now I had one. I wondered who gave it to me. I didn't think it was Justin because he would had given it to me in person. I really didn't know anyone else. Who would give me a Scroll? After thinking for some time, I guessed that some wealthy and loving individual from the Castle had bought it for me. That evening I spent many hours reading. I started at the beginning but then skipped around to other parts.

Just before I went to bed, I came upon a verse that said, *Every warrior is given a special ability for the common good of the army*. This idea fascinated me and I wondered what it meant. What was my special ability? How could I discover it? Early the next morning I found Justin and asked him about it.

"This is what makes the army of the Great King so successful," he explained. "We each have a gifting from above, and it works together with other people's abilities to destroy our enemy."

"But how do you discover your ability?" I asked.

"We should be able to discover yours this coming King's Day," he assured me.

"What is your ability?" I asked.

"Getting people to come to the Castle," he said with a grin. "You are the seventh person that I've convinced to join the army of the Great King."

"That's incredible!" I said. "But how did you know what your ability was?"

"There is a man at the Castle that helps people discover their ability. Don't worry, my friend. Be patient. It will be King's Day before you know it."

King's Day eventually arrived, and with it, my overwhelming desire to discover my ability. Everything about the Castle was as wonderful as before; Captain David delivered a powerful word of courage, the army of the Great King pledged their undying allegiance, and we all heard the words of the Scroll. Immediately after the service, Justin introduced me to a middle-aged man named Eric.

"This is Caleb, and he has just recently chosen to serve the Great King," Justin said. "In his Scroll reading, he discovered that every warrior has an ability and he desires to identify his."

Eric smiled. "How wonderful!" he said. "Come right with me, my dear friend and brother. Let us sit down around this table and visit." I followed him to a small table on the side of the entrance hall. Justin said farewell and went on about his business. Eric made sure I was comfortable and then continued. "This is what I love about the Castle. Everyone has a part to play. None of us are indispensable. I was just remarking, in fact, to our Captain David this very morning that I love seeing people working within their *unique position*, as I call it. This is the joy of my own ability. Oh, what a privilege! Now, my good soldier, I have here a list of many of the main abilities that are here in the Castle. Look over it and let me know if anything stands out to you."

I picked up the parchment he had laid before me and began to read. It was a list of about twenty things. Three of them which immediately caught my eye were *attendants*, *curators*, and *instructors*. I asked him about these.

"Oh yes," he said with delight. "These are some of our more popular abilities. The attendants, as I'm sure you notice every King's Day, are the men and women who help the service flow smoothly. Such people are essential, for without them we wouldn't be able to glean every word from the lips of our captain. And without his words, we will not have the necessary training to slay dragons, and so on and so forth. This might be a very good fit for you, but we must take our time and not be hasty. Regarding the ability of curator, this is also something that we must not take for granted. Look about you, my young man," he said.

I quickly glanced around us at the beautiful polished stone and marble, along with the stained glass. I then looked back at Eric who was smiling with satisfaction at my apparent appreciation for all I saw. "It is beautiful, is it not?" he asked, and continued before I could answer. "If the Castle, and the grounds about it, mind you, are not attractive, well maintained, and beautiful, how can we expect people to be excited about being here? After all, we are servants of the Great King and this is His Castle. What kind of servants would we be if we didn't preserve His Castle and keep it in the most perfect state of being? The curators, therefore, are those who are responsible for the upkeep of all you see here." I nodded with understanding.

"Now," he said. "Regarding the ability of instructor, I'm not sure this would be in line with your path, at least not yet, for the instructor is the one who teaches us about the Great King and His Scroll. Since you are a recent recruit, it would be too soon for you to step into such a position."

"You mean there are others who teach besides Captain David?" I asked curiously.

Eric smiled. "Oh yes. Yes indeed. David teaches at the main gathering, just over there in the Great Hall, but then we have Scroll Class."

"What's Scroll Class?" I asked.

"Why, Scroll Class is where you learn about the Scroll," Eric said with a bit of amazement at my ignorance. "We must get you in such a class right away. But anyhow, as I was saying, it's too early in your training for you to be an instructor."

He then paused, and his eyebrows raised as if an idea had come to him. "Wait a minute!" he said with a smile, as he looked off into the distance. "I have an idea that I think is from the Great King Himself!" He then looked back at me. "How old are you?"

"I am almost twenty," I answered.

"Ha!" he said enthusiastically. "That's it! Have you heard of our Youngling Guild?"

"Youngling Guild?" I repeated. "No, I haven't."

"Well, our Youngling Guild is where we train, obviously, our younglings. Since you are a novice to the army, you are in no place to instruct an adult; however, you are in the perfect position to train a youngling."

"I am?" I said, unsure of how I, a novice, could be able to instruct anyone.

"Absolutely," the man assured me. "These younglings are so important to us. So, so important. After all, they are our future! The issue is that it is so hard for us middle-aged people to speak to them in a way that gets them excited about the Great King. This is why we need someone who is young, but still an adult, if you follow my thinking.

"Yes, you, my dear Caleb, would be perfect for the job. You love the Great King, and yet, you are so nearly plucked from the enemy's camp that you can understand and relate to much of the difficulties and temptations that younglings face. I have tried to talk to them, and they look at me like I'm speaking a foreign language. I have a hard-enough time, ha, speaking to my own younglings about these things. You, however, will be able to make the truths of the Great King relative and exciting, seeing that you speak the correct lingo and are young and attractive. Well, what do you think?"

At this point I was very unsure of what to think. I didn't understand much of what the man was saying, and yet, I did want to be a special part of the Great King's army. And it seemed to me, as I sat there thinking about it, that this was something that most of the army was unable to do since they were older. This was a chance for me to impact the future of the army, seeing as these younglings would be real warriors in a few years. And who knows, maybe one of them would be a future captain!

As I thought it out, I felt more and more excited about the opportunity. I then agreed to the ability, not sure of what it entailed. It turned out that the younglings met twice a week. First, on King's Day, during the main meeting and the adult Scroll Classes, and then again, every Wednesday evening. Seeing as I was a novice, Eric recommended that I serve at the Wednesday meetings, upon which only younglings met. Then I could still be taught by attending the main meeting and the Scroll Class every King's Day. I hardily agreed and was excited to use my ability to serve the Great King.

In the months to come, things only got better. I went to the Castle every King's Day, and I always took my sword with me. I knew that I also needed to become proficient in the bow, but for some reason, my heart was drawn more to the sword, just as it had been in my childhood. Every King's Day, Captain David had amazing words to share, and very often he would open the Scroll. I always felt like his words were spoken directly to me. They always seemed to apply to my life and my need to improve in warfare. Captain David seemed to know everything about the Great King, combat with dragons, and warfare. I quickly decided that I would also master these topics. I always took notes on the messages and reviewed them as often as possible.

I also enrolled in Scroll Class, which took place every King's Day, just after the main Castle meeting. This was more of what I was looking for: training and instruction. We took the Scroll, studied it, and became more proficient warriors.

Justin and I continued to grow closer as friends, and my love for the Great King soared.

My favorite Scroll classes I had taken over those first few months were the following: the history of the sword, how to fletch an arrow, offensive and defensive stances for modern times, and improving your aim. I also learned that the language that the Great King had written the Scroll in was different than our modern language, and so I also learned some of the original words He had spoken. The word *sword* was *ethel*. The *shield* was *bran*. *Dragons* were called *dakel*.

Things were becoming clearer. I was also learning more about the enemy—not only the dragons, but the dragon breeders as well. They were wicked men, who in the secrets of the shadows upon the edges of the forest, would harvest dragon eggs. The local law didn't oppose them, since dragons never exited the forest. But as far as the Castle and the Scroll were concerned, they were enemies.

I asked Justin what that meant. "Do we fight the dragon breeders with the sword?" I asked.

"No," he replied. "The Scroll is clear that our battle isn't against people but dragons. We don't fight the dragon breeders, but we try to open their eyes to the truth; they are in allegiance with the Great Dragon and will therefore never experience the eternal kingdom of the Great King."

"Why would they even want to breed dragons in the first place?" I asked him.

"Dragons are beautiful and mysterious," he explained. "They have the ability to draw you close to them and bring you pleasure. But they will eventually destroy you."

I knew that reality too well, for I had never forgotten the black dragon that lured Lily and I into the forest when we were children.

One day, when Justin and I were leaving the Castle, I noticed the same elderly man I had seen many times before, hooded with a long beard, within the edges of the forest. Even though the distance was long, I felt as if our eyes met.

"Look there!" I said to Justin as I pointed my finger towards the forest. "Do you see that man?!"

The cloaked figure disappeared, but not quickly enough.

"Yes," Justin answered, with disgust in his voice. "I saw him."

"Who is he?" I asked.

Justin looked at me with an expression I had never seen on his face before. "He is our enemy," he said.

Chapter 9

"What do you mean?" I asked. "Is he a dragon breeder?"

"Maybe," he replied. "But he is much worse. He is a backslider, a rebel."

"I've seen him before," I explained. "He makes me uncomfortable. It seems like he's always watching me. What do you mean when you say he is a *backslider*?"

"He used to be part of the Great King's army," Justin explained. "He even trained at the Castle for a time, if I'm not mistaken. I believe it has been many years since he fell back into darkness. Never speak to him. Beware of such people and let him serve as an example. If you don't continue to join others within the Castle, and if you stop training within Scroll Class, you will possibly fall away as well."

"I will never fall away," I replied. "I'm too convinced of these truths."

"I hope you're correct. But remember, the Castle keeps you on the path. That's why the Great King created it."

"That makes sense. I will never abandon the Castle or the Scroll. I will never abandon the Great King."

My Wednesday meetings with the younglings proved to be very enjoyable. We would gather around sundown in the evening and would begin with an activity, such as a competition or team test. Then there was a song and a teaching. I was called upon from time to time to teach and would often share with the younglings the same things that I was learning in Scroll Class. They learned about formations, the history of the dragons, and weaponry. I was teaching the future warriors of the Great King's army. I could think of nothing better. I was like Captain David, only with younglings. I was serving the Great King!

I was also becoming a valuable aid to parents. They would ask me to talk about certain issues with their youngling, issues that were uncomfortable for them to talk about. Other parents felt inadequate since they weren't leaders in the Youngling Guild. I was more and more seen as an expert with younglings. The reality of parenting was becoming clear: parents were called by the Great King to put food on the table, to provide their younglings with shelter and love, and to encourage them to follow the Great King and read the Scroll. But regarding the deeper meaning of the Scroll and its application, they were not often suitable for instructing their younglings; that was my job. Just as the younglings of our village were given to the local tutors to be taught, so also the Castle provided experienced Scroll teachers to speak into the important matters of life. I was finding my place in the kingdom of the Great King, and it was incredible.

One day, as I was working in my shop, Constable Simon came to see me. I was immediately curious about this, for it wasn't Tax Day. His face was burdened with concern and despair. I greeted him in the customary fashion, and skipping all steps of proper etiquette, he shared his thoughts.

"I need your help, Caleb," he said.

"I am at your service," I replied kindly, knowing it was the only way to respond to such a man of influence and power.

"It is a matter that requires discretion," he continued. "I know that I can trust you to remain quiet and not let others in on the situation."

"Your servant is a vault," I said sincerely.

The constable took a deep breath and spoke slowly and quietly. "It is my son, Edgar. I think you know him, or know of him at least. He is a good boy, with encouraging prospects."

"He is around sixteen, is he not?" I asked.

"He is fifteen," he gently corrected me. "And he is my firstborn son. It seems, that despite my best efforts to keep him out of trouble, he has gotten into the wrong crowd. They are a group of thugs and vandals, who not only break the law, but do so in a very crude way. I was hoping you could help him."

I hesitated. The situation seemed a bit too serious for me, a man who had just turned twenty, who had never been tempted to such depths, even in my period of homelessness. But I knew that one doesn't resist the constable—not if they want to keep a low and harmless profile. And what if I failed? Either option was unpleasant to me.

"How could I help him?" I asked.

"You are good with younglings, are you not?" he answered. "Your name came up with another townsperson I was speaking with, only yesterday. I know you serve at the Castle, an embarrassing and utter waste of time in my humble opinion. But if you can keep the younglings from crime and the humiliation of their families, then I suppose some good can come from it."

"I would love to help your son," I said. "I think the best option would be for Edgar to come to the Youngling's meeting, this Wednesday evening. That would be a good first step."

"But my son doesn't believe in the myths of your religion," Simon said with apparent conflict in his heart, for on one hand he disdained the Castle, but on the other hand he was desperate.

"It doesn't matter," I replied kindly and with confidence. "He can come just as he is. It will put him around other younglings of good reputation."

Simon laughed. "You would think so, but I know what really happens when no one is watching."

This statement surprised me. What did he mean? None of our younglings at the Castle got into any trouble. They were all followers of the Great King.

"Very well," Simon said. "I will tell him to go there. I appreciate your help. Whatever it takes, I just need him to stop making such bad decisions. He is wrecking all that I've worked so hard to build."

Simon's son, Edgar, came to the Youngling Guild that Wednesday. At first appearance, I wouldn't have guessed that he was anything other than a well-mannered youngling. He was very respectful and cordial, greeting everyone present and seemingly interested in the program. It turned out that he was already friends with Captain David's son, Joseph, for they played on the same marble team. I was thankful for this; it seemed to make Edgar more comfortable.

The program that evening was to begin with an opening game, a few enjoyable songs, and then end with a testimony by one of our leading younglings, a young girl named Caroline. I was very excited about this new vision of the Youngling Guild: to get our younglings more involved and active in recruiting and training. Caroline was a devout follower of the Great King. She was sixteen years old and was the eldest daughter in a family highly regarded at the Castle. There were about sixty younglings that evening. After our game and music, Caroline began her testimony.

"I have had the privilege of growing up in the Castle," she began. "From my earliest memories, I can remember the Castle walls, the captains, and the Youngling Guild. When I was nine years old, Captain David was assigned to this Castle. I knew, the first time I saw him, that we were going to be a Castle that was pleasing to the Great King. I now read from the Scroll daily. I also take my weaponry with me almost everywhere I go. Some places won't allow me to bring sword or bow, but I have a portion of the Scroll I keep with me always. My greatest desire is to follow the Great King. I am also committed to the purity spoken of in the Scroll: to save

46

myself for my husband, in all manners both physical and emotional. My future plans are to become an adult leader in the Youngling Guild. I may even go to a Great Castle someday. My advice to you is to read the Scroll every day. Find out what you do well and do it for the Great King. He will make His will obvious. Just follow your heart and you won't go astray. If there are some here today that haven't chosen to follow the Great King, come up here and I will pray with you. The Great King is always with us and He knows our hearts."

I was so proud of this young woman. As she spoke, I could feel the Great King with us. For a few seconds, after she ended her testimony, all was quiet. Then, to the surprise and joy of all, Edgar rose to his feet and came forward. Caroline smiled happily and met him with open arms, and on that day, Edgar became a follower of the Great King.

For the rest of that week, I was in high spirits. I reported to Constable Simon, with much pride, the decision his son had made. I was somewhat concerned about his response, seeing as he loathed the Castle, but I didn't care. His son was now my brother, and I was proud of him.

"Well," he said with some indifference, "as long as it helps him stay out of trouble."

That Saturday, as I was heading to the market, I saw many of the older younglings together, as was their custom, and Edgar was with them. His face was beaming with joy. Caroline seemed to be their leader. As I saw them walk along the way, I was struck once again with the satisfaction of serving in the Castle. Here was a score of younglings, all behaving in obedience to the Scroll. They had a strong bond, and as peers, were able to help each other through the dangers and temptations that come with their age. I was only a few years older and could relate to some degree. And Edgar, a youngling who previously was a rebel, was now an honorable soldier of the Great King. If I ever had children, how thankful I would be for the Youngling Guild. My heart broke for parents who didn't have that resource, who were trying to raise their children on their own, whose children would be cursed to settle for the peers of this world instead of kingdom peers. It wasn't a complicated formula: get your children to Scroll School; get them to the Youngling Guild; choose good Castle younglings to be friends for your children.

I arrived at the market and began to set up shop. I had much to do that day, mainly horseshoes and nails, and would need to get to it quickly. I was just beginning to stoke my fire when suddenly, out of nowhere, loud cries filled the air. It was the voice of two young children—one, a boy, the other, a girl—and their cries were coming from the forest. Most of the people on that side of the market stopped their business and began to make for the forest, for the cries were desperate and terrible. Soon the young boy emerged, scratched from head to toe from the briars of the forest, shouting at the top of his lungs.

"Mia!" he shouted, "Mia is trapped!" Some of us took hold of the boy and asked him what he was talking about. "She's trapped!" he continued. "Under the roots of a willow tree!"

We could hear the faint cries of the girl coming from the forest, but they were not alone. Another sound was heard, a deep rumbling, like a strong force scratching away at the earth.

"What is that noise?" I asked.

"The dragon!" the boy shouted hysterically. "The dragon is going to kill her!"

Chapter 10

I was standing back in my childhood nightmare. The imagery of the dragon swallowing the men, Lily's frightened face, it all returned to me at once, nearly causing me to fall to the ground. But I quickly came to my senses. I remembered who I was. I was a warrior of the Great King! All the villagers just looked at each other. They all knew that no one ever entered the forest when a dragon was present, even if a child was in danger; they were too frightened. Fortunately, there were two others from the Castle there with me.

"Grab your weapons!" I said to them.

They looked at me with a petrified gaze.

"Why?" they asked.

I returned an expression of shock and shame. "Because we're going to fight the dragon and save the girl!" I said.

"But shouldn't we get Captain David?" one of them asked.

Captain David... I couldn't deny that the suggestion was a good one. But I knew that there simply wasn't enough time.

"Grab your weapons, and follow me," I said with resolution in my voice. The two men had their weapons with them, for all good followers of the Great King carry their weapons with them everywhere they go. Within only half a minute we were entering the forest.

The sounds were the same: the cries of a young girl, alone and afraid. And the snorts and deep groans of a dragon, likely pawing at the earth, trying to obtain its prize. The men I was with followed me at a steady but removed distance. As I looked back at them, I was perplexed, for they didn't even seem like they knew how to hold their weapons, and yet I knew they had been at the Castle longer than me. One of the men had a bow, while I and the other man had swords. Soon we came upon the scene, and it was just as I imagined.

The dragon was trying to remove a young girl from a protective cage made by the roots of a very strong and old willow tree. The dragon immediately sensed our presence and turned to us. It was an enormous beast. Its red hide was covered like a garment of blood. Its back was rowed with large plates and spikes. Its claws were as long swords, sharp and ready for the kill. The dragon fixed its eyes upon us and began to take in a deep breath.

"Dragon fire!" one of the men shouted. We quickly held up our shields as we ducked behind trunks and logs. To say the fire was hot is an understatement. After the blaze ceased, I looked back to see my two fellow soldiers running away.

"Help!" the girl screamed. I was reminded of Lily, and how I was too late to save her from the fires of that evening so many years earlier. I decided then and there that I would die fighting for this girl. I would not desert her. I turned back to the dragon, who was now looking back at the girl to make sure she hadn't moved. I was about to make my move to strike when I heard a familiar voice. It was Justin.

"Caleb!" he shouted from the edge of the forest. I looked back. I could faintly see him through the foliage.

"Get out of there!" he said. "Captain David is on his way! Wait for reinforcements!"

I turned back to the dragon. No sooner had I refocused upon my foe than my peripheral vision caught the beast's huge tail swinging at me. It was too late. I sailed through the trees, landed upon my back, and nearly blacked out. I soon felt the arms of men grabbing me from the ground and picking me up.

"Must go back," I tried to say.

Justin was one of the men carrying me. "What were you thinking?" he said. Once we were a little way outside the forest's edge, they sat me down upon the ground. I felt like a fool. I looked back at the forest expecting to hear the cries of a girl whose life I couldn't save. But something entirely different happened. I saw the girl, running out of the forest, unscathed by the enemy.

The sight gave me strength and I rose to my feet. Everyone ran to the girl, making sure she was alright and trying to find out what happened.

"It's dead!" she said amidst tears and trembling. "The dragon is dead!" The girl then fell upon the ground, exhausted, and would say no more.

Many of the men, along with myself, timidly entered the forest. We could see the red of the dragon through the thicket, unmoving and quiet.

"It might be a trick," Justin said, his face full of fear.

"Look!" a man said. "Its head has been severed from its body!"

Sure enough, there beside the body of the enormous beast was its head, wretched and lifeless.

"You killed it!" a man said, looking my way.

"I most certainly did not," I replied. "Look. Here is my sword on the ground, where it landed after I was struck by the dragon. It has no blood upon it. I didn't do anything to this dragon."

"Then who did?" another asked.

It was a mystery which none of us there could answer. Captain David and some of his leading men soon arrived. They examined the body but couldn't solve the riddle. In the end, the people of Ravenhill rejoiced, for the dragon was dead and the children were saved.

The next day was King's Day and the Castle was still on a high from the mysterious slaying of a dragon. The first half of Captain David's message was reviewing the event to those who hadn't heard about it.

"As far as who or what killed the dragon," he said. "No one knows, though I think I have a good idea. There were no signs of an army present, and besides, we are the only army for miles. No, my friends, listen to me carefully, for I do not say these words idly. It was not an army, but a soldier who killed that dragon, a single soldier. It was the Great King himself."

The entire meeting hall was silenced, and for a moment, there was a presence of overwhelming awe. Captain David allowed the realization of his statement to sink in and then continued.

"The Great King is trying to get our attention. We should have been ready and able to kill that dragon, but we weren't. The Great King, therefore, came and gave us an example, a sign of encouragement. Listen to the words of the Scroll!"

He then opened the Scroll and read.

Train for battle. Engage the enemy. Be of one mind with your brothers. Kill dragons. He then rolled up the Scroll. "The Scroll says that we are to do these things. This is why we gather. Just the other day, I spoke with a young woman, a wife and mother, concerning her situation. She was not fulfilled in her life. Her heart was empty. *Follow the Great King,* I told her, *and you will find peace.* She is now here with us. The Great King is pleased with us. Let us continue to obey Him and serve Him. And let us follow His example! Listen to me, my brothers and sisters, and hear this great news: in one week from today, on the next King's Day, we will all travel to the edges of the great forest. And there, we will kill a dragon!"

Everyone cheered and rejoiced at this announcement. I, especially, was thrilled. I wouldn't be beaten back again by a dragon. This time I would encounter the dragon, side-by-side with my captain and brother, and I would be victorious. I went home that day and sharpened my sword. The next King's Day, we were going to kill a dragon!

Chapter 11

Everyone was bustling about with excitement throughout the week. Captain David and his lead soldiers were making the final plans and strategies for the hunt. Many were also planning for the celebration dinner that would follow the battle. A special meeting for the leaders of the younglings was called. Every youngling was to stay within or close proximity to the Castle. Allowing them to be within range of the forest was too dangerous. We were fortunately able to find enough adult leaders who would shepherd the younglings, making it possible for me to attend the slaying. That King's Day everyone arrived at the Castle on time and excitement filled the air.

Captain David stepped up to the podium and opened the Scroll. "Within the Scroll, we read the following: *You will advance in My name, and the dragons will not overcome you. You will fight with sword and bow and will be victorious.* This is what we will now do! Clutch your swords! Ready your bows! We march to the forest!"

Everyone shouted in unison, and the march began. I quickly made sure that all of the younglings and their leaders were accounted for and then hurried on to join the army. Justin was next to me as we marched. Songs were sung and truths from the Scroll were proclaimed. Everyone chose that day their preferred weapon, and therefore assembled as archers and sword-wielders. I chose the sword, as was my preference. We then reached the edge of the forest and awaited orders. We were nearly four-hundred in number.

Captain David's voice broke the silence. "Form the defense of the crescent moon!" We all knew what this meant and how to do it and were within only a moment aligned as a crescent moon, with the opening of the arch facing the tree line of the forest. Archers were on the left and right flank with those wielding the sword in the middle. Captain David sent out his two most trusted commanders to inspect the ranks, who then reported back to David that all was in order.

Captain David then took his position within the opening of the formation, closest to the forest, with both commanders on either side. He opened the Scroll and read aloud, "*The Great Dragon, and his offspring are doomed for destruction!*" All of the army responded in unison, "Amen!" Captain David then continued reading, "*We are the army of the Great King!*" Again we all responded, "Amen!" Then Captain David and his two commanders unsheathed their swords and began to march towards the forest.

"Are we allowed to enter the forest with them?" I asked Justin, who was beside me.

"Only if they ask for assistance," he replied.

"Has that ever happened?" I continued.

"Not that I know of. Remember, Captain David has been to one of the Great Castles. He is trained for this more than anyone present."

The answer satisfied me, to a degree, for I remembered my last experience trying to fight a dragon. We then heard a roar that seemed to shake the earth beneath us. Everyone gasped in fear.

"What was that?" I asked, though I knew the answer.

"It was a dragon," replied Justin with a hint of fear in his voice. "Do you still want to enter the forest?"

"Not at all," I answered.

"Exactly," he said, with a tone of justification. "This is why we have captains."

I looked around me to see how my fellow soldiers were faring when I noticed something that took me completely off guard. There was a man, not much older than myself, out of formation, and a little behind the army. The first thing that drew me to him was that he was out of formation, and yet, he was clearly a warrior for the Great King. I could see it in his eyes, not to mention his sword and shield which were strapped upon his back and side. He was a warrior, and yet, he looked different—like he was one of us but not the same as us. The main thing, however, that made him stand out was that he had with him two younglings. I quickly broke out of formation and approached him.

"Excuse me," I said as I approached. The man looked at me with a look of both kindness and soberness mixed together. I continued, "I'm sorry to have to tell you this, but these younglings cannot be here."

The man smiled and looked down at the two boys, who I then noticed were both armed with swords, not ones made out of paper or wood but real metal swords!

"Why can't my two sons be here?" the man gently asked.

"It's too dangerous," I replied, glancing back to the forest where the roar had come from. "I am a leader of the younglings and must request that they all stay at the Castle, where they will be safe."

"I see," the man replied. "That's very interesting. With all due respect, it is more dangerous for you to be here than these boys. As for your comment regarding the Castle, I will hold my tongue."

The man's words confused me, and I honestly didn't understand what he was saying. Then another roar filled the air, mixed with the sounds of Captain David and his two commanders shouting. Everyone gasped again. We then saw movement ahead, as if something was coming out of the forest. It was bright red, the very color we all dreaded. It was blood red, the color of a dragon.

Everyone took a step back, and some even turned to run. But then we all recognized the face of Captain David, along with his two commanders. They were carrying together the head of a dragon. Everyone let out a shout of relief and joy. Captain David smiled, as best he could, for he seemed sapped of all energy as were his two commanders, who were both cut and bruised. Together they held high the head of the dragon, while Captain David shouted, "Victory!"

Everyone rejoiced again and immediately surrounded their Captain with embraces, adoration, and thanksgiving. Soon tables and chairs were put in place and food and drink were served. As I was making my way toward Captain David, to give him my thanks, I then remembered the man and the younglings. I looked back and could still see them, though they were walking away from the celebration. My emotions regarding this man were mixed; I was frustrated, curious, and inspired all at the same time. I quickly ran toward the man and got his attention.

"Wait!" I called out. The man turned to me. "Won't you come celebrate with us?" I asked him.

"Celebrate?" the man replied. "What is there to celebrate?"

"The slaying of a dragon!" I said with a bit of frustration in my voice.

The man looked toward the festivities, sighed, and then looked to me. "Forgive me, friend. The slaying of a dragon is worthy of rejoicing, but one slain dragon does not outweigh the sad reality of all I have seen here today."

I was about to ask him what he meant when I felt a hand on my shoulder. It was Justin.

"Come, my friend," he said with excitement. "We are now allowed to sink our swords and arrows within the carcass."

I slowly turned around at the urging of my friend. After only thirty or so paces, I looked back toward the stranger and the younglings, but they were gone. He had told me that something he saw there saddened him. But what was it? We killed a dragon. Was he a dragon breeder?

"I really wanted to talk to that man," I told Justin. "He said things that didn't make sense to me. It was as if he knew something that I didn't."

"Don't ever talk to him again," insisted Justin, as we hurried back to the celebration. "He's one of the backsliders."

I hoped that the celebration would get my mind off of the backslider I had just encountered. The only problem was, he didn't seem like a backslider. There was something about him that seemed just the opposite. I was, fortunately, brought back to the joy of the Castle when I got to sink my sword into the body of the dragon. However, I was surprised at the size of the creature. It was much smaller than the dragons I had previously seen. The body was only about eight feet in length and the head was no larger than a horse's head.

Caroline's parents then approached me.

"Caleb," her father said with love and friendship, "what a wonderful celebration this is, eh? I can't wait until Caroline is of age so she can enjoy it, but I understand that if they aren't ready, they aren't ready. I do, however, have a matter of concern I want to discuss with you. My daughter has become very good friends with Edgar, and as you know, he is the son of Simon, a very powerful man in the community with much potential for family prosperity. I see this as a wonderful opportunity for my family, but I also have questions. What does the Castle teach regarding the relationship between a young man and a young woman? Edgar is a very recent member of the Castle. Is that an issue? Any help you have would be much appreciated. Caroline respects you dearly, as do we all."

The situation and questions were racing through my mind, and I had no good answers. I had never even considered relationships within the Castle. I knew how the world did such things, but surely the Castle was different.

"Wait here one moment," I said to the man, and quickly returned with Susanna, who was the head of the Youngling Guild. I posed to her the question, and she counseled Caroline's parents at that very moment.

"What an exciting time," she began with a smile. "There is nothing that gets me more excited than seeing younglings, at this appropriate age, start to develop linking relationships. It has become obvious to me, in only this very short time, that Edgar and Caroline are kindred spirits. That is, of course, as long as you approve of the match?" She then paused in order to see his reply.

"Well, of course I approve, contingent on the fact that the boy continues coming to both the Castle's Youngling Guilds as well as other weekly gatherings."

"Of course," echoed Susanna. "Your daughter is a gem that requires nothing short of such standards. They will naturally be linking soon, if they aren't already."

"Naturally," the father replied, with not as much confidence in his voice. "But what exactly does that look like? I know how the world does linking. How does the Castle link? Not the way of the world I suppose?"

"Of course not," agreed Susanna. "The world links in such a wicked way. As it is written, *we are not of this world, and so we do things differently*. The guidelines are simple. First, the couple mustn't stay out past a certain curfew, such as ten o'clock or so. They must commit, most of all, to coming to all gatherings of the Youngling Guild, and must be involved in leadership positions."

"But young Edgar is such a recent convert," I interrupted. "Is he ready for leadership?"

Susanna looked at me with a hint of frustration. "My dear Caleb, how long have you been a follower of the Great King? Look at all you have done for the Castle. The issue isn't one of maturity but heart and talent, and young Edgar has both." She then continued with Caroline's father.

"And now, sir, we come to the most sensitive part. Many parents in the Castle fear what physical measures will be compromised in such relationships." The father nodded in eager agreement.

"We mustn't put unrealistic expectations on our younglings," she said. "That only breeds rebellion. That is why we put physical boundaries on all couples but not boundaries that are unrealistic. We allow them to hold hands, and they get one kiss goodnight."

"That is ridiculous!" the father exclaimed. "Why, when I was a youngling we didn't do anything like that!"

Susanna smiled. "Times have changed, sir. These ideas of physical boundaries aren't something we came up with. They are from the Great Castles. All Youngling Guilds, within every Castle in this area, are doing such things. We have other couples that are linking and following these guidelines, and with little exception, all is going well. Remember, sir, this is why you have us. We have the latest training, given to us by the greatest sages of the Scroll."

Chapter 12

I decided to get an early start at the shop the following morning. Being a blacksmith, I always enjoyed the cooler months of the year, for the crisp breeze would bring a welcomed relief to the heat of the fire. As I took a brief break, around mid-day, I noticed him. It was the man from the dragon slaying, the man who was with the two boys and then disappeared. I was again drawn to something in his countenance. He seemed free, even more so than my companions at the Castle. I was thankful when he decided to visit my shop.

"Good morning," he said cheerfully. I returned the gesture. He then continued. "I'm looking for some horseshoes, medium sized."

"I have many," I replied, but I did not get them. Instead, I continued to look at him. "You are the man from the slaying, aren't you? I saw you with the two boys. Do you remember me?"

"Of course I remember you," he said with a kind smile. "And yes, that was me, with my sons."

"Are you a follower of the Great King?" I asked him.

"Indeed I am," he replied. "And you?"

"Yes, sir," I answered. "Forgive me for being so bold, but why did you have your younglings with you at the slaying?"

"Why shouldn't they be there?" the man replied.

"Because it's dangerous," I replied.

"Indeed it is," the man said with a laugh. "But dangerous to whom? Those who are young, or those who can't wield their weapon proficiently?"

These questions stumped me, for in all my study I had found nothing in the Scroll that distinguished younglings and warriors, though the Castle made such distinctions.

"Are you new to this area?" I asked.

"Oh no. I have been here since my childhood."

"I wonder why I never see you?" I continued. "What Castle do you attend?"

"I don't go to any Castle," the man replied kindly.

"You don't go to a Castle?" I replied with confusion. I couldn't help but stare awkwardly at the man, for he seemed like no one I had ever known. "I'm sorry," I said at last, "but I don't understand."

"Do not be troubled," he said. "You wonder how I can be a follower of the Great King and not go to a Castle?"

"Yes, exactly," I said with gratitude.

The man nodded his head. "Your question is good and deserves an answer. But let me, after the example of the Great King, answer your question with another question."

I was taken off guard a bit by this, but the man's gentleness forced me to comply. "Very well," I said.

"Are you able to use your sword?" the man asked.

"Am I able to use my sword?" I repeated thoughtfully, as I reached over and took hold of it. I held it in front of him with a friendly smile. "Of course I am."

The man continued with his gentle interview. "So, you're saying that you've trained on how to wield it?"

"Absolutely," I replied. I began to see that this was the consequence of people who don't go to a Castle. They obviously know little and miss out. I then grabbed some of my notes and showed them to him.

"Look at this," I said, hoping he was literate. "Here are sketches of different types of swords. And here are different ways of sharpening them. I've also been trained in the art of the bow."

"The bow?" he said curiously.

"Yes, of course. The bow is a deadly tool against the dragons."

"And you, a man, wields the bow?" he questioned.

"I prefer the sword," I said. "But I am also proficient with the bow."

"Interesting," he replied, "that you, as a man, would wield the bow."

"Why is that interesting?" I probed.

The man shook off the topic. "Never mind that," he said. "My original question still stands: have you actually trained?"

I was getting more and more confused and a bit frustrated. I referred again to my notes. "Look here. I know all about warfare with dragons."

The man continued in both kindness and patience. "I know you know about swords. I know you know the techniques. I know that you could teach others everything you know. But I'm asking about actually doing it, out there. Are you able to actually hold the sword in your hand, wield it, and kill a dragon?"

These questions made me angry, for I knew that the overarching answer was *no*. And suddenly, my anger was replaced with confusion. I realized at that moment that even though I knew about swords and bows and formations, I had no idea how to actually engage the enemy. I realized that amidst all the lessons and classes, I was never actually trained. I felt I owed the man a response.

"I've never been to a Great Castle," I said.

"A Great Castle?" the man repeated. He then looked at me thoughtfully. "Are you a Scroll reader?"

"Of course."

"Then I give you one last question before I leave you in peace. Have you seen any mention of the Great Castles in the Scroll?"

The man then bowed. "My name is Nathan. Farewell."

"But wait!" I said desperately, longing for more information.

He simply turned and smiled sincerely before he continued on his way. "Consult the Scroll, my friend. We will meet again."

I quickly closed down my shop, though the day was young, picked up my notes and ran in the direction of Justin's house.

As I ran to Justin's house, my mind was racing. We had been taught in Scroll Class that we should always be able to defend our faith and traditions. And yet, this man asked simple questions for which I had no answers. He made me feel foolish. I knew that pride was a root of darkness and that I must not let my inability to answer his questions make me doubt things. I was obviously still a novice warrior and had much to learn. There was nothing wrong with the Castle and how we did things. The problem was just my lack of understanding. Now I would get the correct answers from Justin. I found him in his father's garden, for the harvest was near.

"Greetings, brother!" he exclaimed as he saw me.

"Justin!" I shouted. "I have questions!"

My friend noticed the distressed look on my face. "What's wrong?" he asked. "Did something bad happen?"

"Do you remember the man from the slaying, who had his sons with him?"

Justin nodded.

"I spoke with him in the market just now, and his words confused me."

Justin suddenly looked angry. "I told you not to talk to him! He's a backslider. That's what they do. His goal is to turn you away from the Castle."

"Really?" I asked. "Are you sure?"

"Absolutely," Justin confirmed. "They are part of the problem and not the solution. Don't talk to him ever again."

"Alright," I said, but I doubted my response. I desperately wanted to talk to that man, Nathan, again. "Well," I continued, "nevertheless, I have questions."

"What are they?" Justin asked, still a bit frustrated.

"Why don't we train? Like, really train? I've never seen an archery range or any real training arena at the Castle."

"What do you mean?" Justin asked.

"It's a simple question," I said kindly but with desperation. "We are soldiers of the Great King, and we know a lot of information, but we don't really go out there and fight dragons. We talk about it. We sing about it. We learn about it. But we don't do it. Why don't we actually pick up our weapons and learn how to wield them?

"Caleb," Justin replied with a laugh, "you should really go to a Great Castle. It seems you're called to pursue that. All those things are at the Great Castles. That's why Captain David is the great warrior he is."

I stood thoughtfully. Maybe he was right. Maybe all of my frustration was just the Great King revealing that I was supposed to go above and beyond the other warriors. Perhaps I was called to be a captain and lead my own Castle. I imagined myself like Captain David, leading my own army to the edge of a forest, entering by myself, and coming back with the head of a dragon. Everyone would rejoice and look at me and see me as a true warrior of the Great King. Maybe I would even train some of them up to go into the forest with me. A smile formed on my face. I looked back at Justin, who was also smiling.

"Do you really think so?" I asked. "Do you really think I should go to a Great Castle and become a captain?"

"Without a doubt," he replied. "Why else would you be so passionate about training and fighting? You should talk to Captain David, for he will be able to get you into the right one."

I pondered it all some more, and then my mind was resolute. After all, this is what I had been dreaming of ever since Lily and I pretended together as children. I had always wanted to slay dragons, and now I had a plan to accomplish that dream. I would become a captain.

"Thank you, my friend," I said to Justin. "Everything makes sense now."

"My pleasure," he replied. "The Great King is leading you. And remember, stop talking to the backsliders; they will only confuse and distract you."

I turned back toward the market with a smile on my face. Still, something Nathan the backslider said kept echoing in my mind. He had asked me, *Does the Scroll speak of Great Castles?* I repeated the question a few times in my mind, then I did my best to erase it. Nothing would hold me back. I was going to one of the Great Castles. I was going to become a captain!

Chapter 13

I didn't return to the market that day, for the more I thought about the Great Castle and me becoming a captain, I just had to see Captain David right away. I set my steps now towards the Castle, for he was usually there. As I passed by the great forest, I thought I saw that old, hooded man appear and then quickly disappear back within the trees. *Backsliders,* I thought. I was beginning to build up a hostility in my heart towards them. *Their questions and their rebellion make too much trouble. They may even be dragon breeders,* I said to myself.

I then reached the Castle and was pleased to find Captain David.

"Caleb," he said with a smile that made my heart glow. "How's my favorite warrior doing today?"

"Doing great!" I replied. "I have something to tell you."

"Oh yes? And what is that?"

"I want to go to a Great Castle and become a captain like you!"

The expression on Captain David's face was a bit disheartening. He initially, for only a second, had a look on his face which seemed to show doubt or even disapproval concerning my idea. He quickly covered it back up with a smile.

"Captain Caleb," he said with joy in his voice. "What a wonderful thing that would be!"

"Could you get me into a Great Castle?" I asked hopefully.

He hesitated, and I'm sure he could see the disappointment on my face.

"In time," he replied. "This is a long process, very long I'm afraid. You've only been a warrior now for how long? Around six months? There are still warriors who have been training here for years who are not ready for the Great Castles."

These words stirred up everything within me that Nathan questioned. I was now back where I was before I spoke with Justin. I was being emotionally and mentally tossed back and forth and didn't know what way was right and wrong. My mouth suddenly and without warning blurted out the following: "Why don't we ever train? Really train? Why don't we ever shoot bows at targets for instance?"

Captain David looked at me curiously. "What do you mean? We train all the time. At the Fall Festival, we have an archery contest. Didn't you know that? Besides, you can always shoot at targets on your own time."

The answer wasn't satisfactory in the least.

"But aren't we supposed to be killing dragons?" I asked. "Not just marching out with you to watch you slay dragons, but actually killing them?"

I could see the frustration forming on Captain David's face; then he softened a bit and smiled. "You have the heart of a captain," he said. "I understand what you are asking, and I hope you are able to accept my answer: you still have much to learn. Remember, you are new to all of this. I am your captain. You must trust me. If I let all of the members of this Castle march into the forest, what would that look like? How many people would be lost or beaten? They would lose heart. The Castle would empty. Can you imagine what it would look like every King's Day? So, you just take time to be still. Don't be rash. Keep coming to the Castle. Keep attending Scroll Class. You will learn, just as many others have, how this all works."

I took a deep breath and nodded my head. I had nothing to say; I was emotionally drained. Captain David placed his hand upon my shoulder, tried his best to encourage me, and sent me on my way. I slowly walked back to my home, my mind racing through all that had happened in the last two days. I remembered the words of Nathan, Justin, and Captain David. The one phrase, however, that wouldn't leave my mind was from Nathan:

Consult the Scroll, he had told me. Consult the Scroll.

It was now close to sunset as I made my way back to my home. I was emotionally and mentally exhausted. I was looking forward to an early sleep, which would hopefully result in a clear head when morning came. I was walking past the edges of the forest when I saw not one cloaked figure, as usual, but five. They were walking within the shadows of the forest, and two of them were carrying a large container of some kind. My curiosity got the best of me and I followed them. The darkness of evening drew near, making it hard to see the cloaked figures as they continued to walk along the edge of the forest. Fortunately, by the glow of the moon, I was able to keep up with them. I then saw them enter the forest, something I wasn't willing to do. I waited by the edge of the trees, crouched low and a little frightened. I then noticed the tender glow of a fire, only a stone's throw within the forest. I slowly crawled within the thicket and approached close enough to where I could see what was happening.

The five figures were circled around a fire and were all cloaked so as to conceal their faces. The container they had looked like a crate, covered with a cloth of some kind with two poles extending out of each side for carrying. I could smell strong drink in the air and assumed that it was from them.

"Are you sure no one knows we are here?" said one.

"Positive," said another. "No one comes close to the forest at night."

"Well, let's hurry up," said a third. "I'm always nervous being here."

"You shouldn't be," said another. "The dragons won't hurt us. We are on their side."

He then reached over and pulled the cloth off of the cage. Inside was a baby dragon. My heart nearly burst out of my chest! I couldn't believe it. They were dragon breeders. The young dragon was only about three feet from head to tail. After one of the dragon breeders unlatched the cage, he removed his hood. I was astonished to recognize the young man, though I wondered if I was dreaming. It was Joseph, Captain David's son!

Even though Joseph was in the Youngling Guild, I hadn't gotten to know him well, for he was quiet and reserved. I had noticed that the relationship between he and his father was a bit divided, but I would have never imagined that he was a dragon breeder.

"Well done, Judas," Joseph said, motioning to another hooded figure sitting across from him. "This is the most beautiful dragon you've ever bred. Indeed, I've never seen anything like it before."

Judas seemed to nod in response. Joseph continued, "It breaks my heart that my father and others in the Castle speak of killing these creatures. They all think them evil and bad, but it's a lie. Look." He then reached within the cage and held the dragon in his arms. "The dragons aren't evil," he continued. "They will not destroy you unless you are prejudiced against them and a weakling. They will actually make you stronger. Now, it is time for each of you to hold and embrace the dragon."

Joseph then handed the dragon to the person next to him. The stranger removed his hood, and again, I was taken aback. It was Edgar! He laughed with foolish pride. "I am not afraid of this dragon," he said as he held it and petted its head. "I will never kill such an amazing creation." He then looked to the figure next to him. "You don't have to do this if you're afraid."

"I'm not afraid," the person said. The moment she spoke, I knew her voice, and my heart shuttered. It was Caroline.

Chapter 14

I remained in my position, petrified with fear and confusion. I didn't know what to do. I wanted to shout out at them all. I wanted to run away. To my shame and horror, all I could do was remain still, lying upon the ground and watching. Four of the five individuals had passed the dragon around, all taking turns caressing the beast and pledging loyalty to its race.

It was now Caroline's turn to hold the dragon. She hesitated. "Are you sure this is alright?" she asked with trepidation in her voice. "I'm afraid that this is wrong, that we are going against the Scroll."

Edgar put his arm around her. "Sweetheart," he said gently, "we have already talked about this. Look at this beautiful dragon. Would the Great King make something as wonderful as this to be destroyed, or embraced? Joseph is also here. You told me that you were all in, that I could count on you. You told me that you would follow me and trust me. Don't I have your heart?"

I shuddered as I watched this unfold. I saw Caroline look at Edgar as he gave her a kiss.

"Yes," she said. "You have my heart."

She then took hold of the dragon, and as she did, a smile came across her face and excitement shone from her eyes. And it was as if her eyes were empty, that they were void of any presence of the Great King.

"This is so amazing!" she said. I noticed Edgar and Joseph look at each other and smile. She then passed the dragon on to Joseph.

"And now we set you free," Joseph declared to the young beast. "But remember us and be kind to us."

As the group let the creature go, I noticed a slight movement off to my right. It was another cloaked figure, creeping closer to the group. They didn't seem to notice him. I then caught a glimpse of hair coming out of the opening of the cloak. Long hair, like a beard. The first person I thought of was the old man. Perhaps he was their leader. Now it was all coming together. The backslider that Justin had identified to me was a dragon breeder, who lurked on the edges of the forest, luring young people to his evil practice. I didn't know what to do. Again, I was petrified with fear.

The figure then stopped and went to one knee, and I again saw the hair. It wasn't white but red. This wasn't the old man. The stranger then removed a bow and arrow and took aim towards the group.

Before I had a chance to say anything, the arrow sprang from the stranger's bow and sank deep into the neck of the dragon. The group of dragon breeders cried aloud in shock and surprise. I rose to my feet and began to run away as fast as I could. I heard a loud shout from within the forest. I didn't recognize it, and guessed it to be Judas, the dragon breeder who Joseph praised. "No!" he shouted. "How could you?! I will kill you for this!" I didn't look back, but kept running until I reached my home.

I awoke the next morning, hoping that all I had seen was just a nightmare. But I knew that it had really happened. Three people that I had great admiration for—Joseph, Edgar, and Caroline—all turned out to be engaged in enemy activity. I didn't know who Judas was or the identity of the fifth stranger, but I wondered if they had ever attended the Youngling Guild. And who was the cloaked stranger who killed the dragon? The only hint I had was red hair.

Just like most days, I was supposed to go to the market. But I was unable to. My mind was too conflicted. There were a few issues that had to be resolved. I took the Scroll, opened it, and prayed.

Oh, Great King, I know that You can hear me. Please erase everything I think I know and teach me anew from Your word. I want the truth, no matter what it means I must change. I want the truth, no matter what others will think. Please, oh, Great King, please teach me the truths of Your Kingdom. Amen.

The Scroll was long and had many parts, much of which I hadn't even read yet. I simply began reading. For many hours I just read. I then remembered Nathan thinking it odd that I wielded the bow. Why was that? I knew that if there was a reason, it would be in the section of the Scroll titled, *Concerning Swords and Bows.* I quickly came to that section and began reading. I then found a passage that made my eyes open wide and my heart skip. I couldn't believe what I was reading, and what was more shocking, I had read it many times, in Scroll Class of all places! This is what it said: *In the army of the Great King, only men are permitted to wield the sword, and only women are permitted to wield the bow.*

I was astonished! Why hadn't I recognized this? It was right there in front of me the entire time! It made me wonder what else I might have missed in the Scroll. If I could overlook such an obvious thing as this, I could overlook all kinds of things. Then an answer came to me, from deep within my soul. *You aren't finding My Kingdom because you are led by the practice of those around you instead of by My Scroll.* Was that the Great King speaking to me? I quickly penned the words so I wouldn't forget them.

It was soon King's Day, and I made my way to the Castle. Things were beginning to change, and the change frightened me. For many months, I had felt uncomfortable in the world but comfortable at the Castle. Now, however, both places made me feel uneasy. Everything looked different. As I attended the service, I kept asking myself, *What are we accomplishing here?* and *What are we doing?* Whereas before I saw a great army, training for war against the enemy, I now saw a misguided group of people who *thought* they were a mighty army and *thought* they were training, but who indeed were only fooling themselves. I did not feel like the Great King was smiling upon this gathering. I hoped I was wrong, but I was quickly becoming convinced. After the service, before I made my way to Scroll Class, I approached Captain David. I was so afraid to confront him with what was on my mind. I was so afraid of his disapproval and that he would see me as a troublemaker. But I had to ask him. I had to hear his answer.

"Ah, Caleb," he said with a smile as I approached. I did my best to return the kind gesture.

"Forgive me, Captain," I began. "I know this isn't the best time. I just have one quick question to ask you."

"Of course," he said with his usually kindness. "What is it?"

"I found this passage," I said. I then showed him the passage in the Scroll. "It says here that only men wield the sword, and only women are to wield the bow, and yet here everyone is able to do both. Why is that?"

I could tell that he was trying to hide the frustration etched upon his face. He forced a smile, "Ah, Caleb. You are quite the student. Again, this will all make sense in time. You must understand that much has changed since the Great King first wrote the Scroll."

"But isn't this timeless?" I asked. "Isn't this something dealing with the Great King's creation, and not some outdated practice?"

Captain David sighed and made no more effort to smile. "Caleb, you still have much to learn about the Great King. Who am I to tell a woman she can't wield the sword? If she is gifted that way, it would be wrong to deny her that talent. Or if you,

75

for example, were better gifted with the bow than the sword, how cruel would that be to force you to learn the more difficult weapon? Can you imagine what this place would look like if I said to people, *You can't wield the weapon of your choice. You must do it this way or that way?*"

"Yes," I began. "But if the Scroll plainly says..."

"Enough," Captain David demanded. "That is all for now. As you said yourself, this isn't the best time. I have given you my answer, and I would suggest that you go on to Scroll Class and continue learning instead of trying to answer."

He then turned and continued down the corridor. I was left, once again, confused and frustrated. More than anything, I felt rejected by the one man in the world whose approval I desired most, and I feared not being able to get it back. I wondered if Captain David knew that his son was a dragon breeder. Likely not. But he had to know something wasn't right with his son. Joseph was continually at marble tournaments and hanging out with his peers. I hardly ever saw him with his parents, and I never saw him at the Castle on King's Days. I continued on to Scroll Class but not before checking in on my leaders in the Youngling Guild.

"Everything is in order," said Martha, one of my assistants. "We have the puppets for the youngling show all ready. We are also going to have them fold paper swords and shields and paint them. Their parents will love it."

"Very well," I replied with little enthusiasm. "Just make sure they learn something, will you?"

Martha looked at me crossly. "Of course, they will learn something," she declared. "They learn something every King's Day!" She then turned and walked back to the younglings. Another person I had seemingly offended.

As I walked into Scroll Class, I did my best to hide my confusion, frustration, and disappointment. One part of my heart was frustrated at the ever-increasing chasm between the Castle and the Scroll. Another part of my heart was worried that my dearest friends were thinking me an annoying fool. And yet, most of my heart simply hungered above all else to know the truth.

"Alright everyone, let's get started," began my teacher, Mr. Gabriel. He then noticed my expression which I was trying to hide. "Caleb, is every alright?"

"Yes, sir," I replied, "just having one of those days."

"Well, I hope that this class will encourage you," he said kindly. He then addressed all of those present. "Today we are going to be looking at what the Scroll says about family. This isn't a topic that is discussed much these days, but it is, after all, an important subject. And when we look within the Scroll, there is more there about family than you might think. So, let us open our Scrolls to the book of 'Foundations of Training.'"

My spirits were lifted a bit at this, for of all the books within the Scroll, this was one that I had studied least. Also, for some reason which I did not understand at the time, the topic of family was more and more taking a hold upon my mind and spirit. I wondered if it was because of the image of Nathan and his two sons, all armed together as warriors, which kept burning within my mind. I was also thinking about marriage more than ever before.

The teacher continued. "As you all know, the family is made up of four different roles. There is the husband, the wife, the parents, and the child. The Great King has given us instructions for each of these. You must know these answers. Remember, it also says in the Scroll that *without knowledge, no victory can be attained.* So please pay attention.

"Let us look at the husband," he continued. "The husband is to be the leader of his family. As it says in 'Foundations and Training,' chapter three, verse five: *The husband is the captain of his family.*"

Mr. Gabriel continued the teaching, but I was stuck, dead in my tracks, at the words I just read. *The husband is the captain of his family.* It was the first time I had heard the word *captain* used in any other context than that of the Castle. What did it mean? I quickly fixed my attention back on Mr. Gabriel. "This is why the husband must get his family to the Castle as often as the doors are open," he explained. "The Great King has provided teachers, captains, and mentors for the Castle members, and it is the father's job to get his family where they can receive the training they need. Even now, in the Younglings Guild, your children are learning about the Great King from experts who have been trained in working with younglings in this current age."

"Wait," I said calmly yet firmly. The word left my mouth before I was able to hold it back. All eyes in the class were on me.

"Yes?" asked Mr. Gabriel politely.

"Well" I said, pausing to clear my throat. I was breathing a bit more heavily than I would have preferred. I glanced around at everyone, then looked at the Scroll, and took another deep breath. "Forgive me," I said, "it's just that, well, I've never heard this before and I find it very interesting."

"Yes, it is very interesting indeed," Mr. Gabriel said kindly, not sure whether to let me speak more or continue teaching. A part of me desired for him to go on, and for all eyes to go back to him, but I had to share my mind.

"I was just wondering," I said quickly, "since the Scroll refers to the husband as a *captain*, why don't husbands do the things in their home that Captain David does here? I mean, why don't we see husbands actually training their families?"

Everything was quiet. Some people, with quizzical brows, turned their gaze to Mr. Gabriel while others looked back at their Scrolls. Mr. Gabriel seemed to be thinking through the comment. He then scratched his chin, took a deep breath, and spoke. "That's a very good question," he began. "I suppose that it would be good for husbands to do such things as you are suggesting, though, I'm not sure what that would look like."

"But, sir," someone else in the class interrupted politely, "Caleb isn't *suggesting* that husbands take up the role of captains in the home. It is thus *stated* in the

Scroll. So then, this isn't a suggestion of the Great King but rather a command, is it not? Doesn't this mean that husbands are commanded to shepherd their families?"

"Well," replied Mr. Gabriel with a smile, "you've definitely got me there. I mean, if the Scroll says it, it's true and it's good and we should do it. So, I suppose it would be a good idea for husbands to do things with their families that Captain David does with us."

"Such as what?" asked another student. "What things would a husband do that Captain David does? Surely you don't expect them to preach to their families?"

"No, no," replied Mr. Gabriel, "of course not. That would require a measure of training that only happens at the Great Castles. But I do suppose it would be good to read the Scroll to their families, just as Captain David does to us."

There was a feeling of uneasiness in the room, and I believed that everyone could sense it. We all knew that virtually no husband in our Castle ever sat down with their family, opened the Scroll, and read. And yet, at the suggestion, it sounded so simple. And not only simple, but obvious. Why wouldn't a husband read the Scroll to his wife and children? At the time, I couldn't think of anything better for a husband to do. I wondered how my first twenty years would have looked different if my father had read the Scroll to me. It was still quiet in the room, and I assumed everyone was having similar conversations in their minds.

"Mr. Gabriel," I finally said, "if it is the husband's role, as the captain of his family, to train up his family, then why do we have the Youngling Guild? In other words, is the Youngling Guild found in the Scroll?"

Again, all was quiet. Poor Mr. Gabriel just sat there, staring off into space with a confused look on his face as if he was trying to remember his own name.

"No," he said at last. "It isn't mentioned by name. Indeed, when the Great King wrote the Scroll, there was no such thing as the Youngling Guild, nor was there in the many centuries of the early Castles. We definitely do things a bit differently now than they did back then."

"Yes," chimed in one of the mothers of a child in the Youngling Guild. "But just because they didn't do it back then doesn't mean it's a bad thing. I mean, who's to say that we haven't evolved in our understanding since then, even to a point where we could do it better than they did?"

"Do it better than the Great King and His first soldiers?" asked another with a tone of shock and offense.

Mr. Gabriel quickly interrupted, "Thank you everyone for those wonderful comments. It is always a good thing to think about what the Scroll says and how it can play out in our daily lives. Yes, yes. Let us move on now to our next role: the role of parents. In the same chapter, in verse eight, it reads, *Fathers, train your children in the warfare of the Great King'*" Mr. Gabriel's words drifted off as he came to the last words of the verse, for it seemed to catch him in a different light, likely due to the conversation we were having.

He sighed. "Well, it seems that this definitely backs up the idea Caleb presented," he said with a chuckle. "Hmmm. It sure is interesting how verses can read a different way depending on the context. There's no Youngling Guild in that verse, is there?" He then paused for a while as he was scanning his notes. "Well, class, I think we are going to be letting you out a bit early today. I suppose I wasn't quite as prepared as I normally am. Anyhow, thanks for coming, and I look forward to seeing you next week."

Chapter 15

I quickly exited the Scroll Class and went out into the main hall. Caroline and Edgar were there, holding hands and talking to some of their friends. Their faces were radiant, so it seemed. To all others, they looked like two devoted followers of the Great King. I was pleased to see that they hadn't been harmed by the archer from the previous evening, but my heart broke at the same time to see their inappropriate affection for each other—not to mention the knowledge I had that they were dragon breeders. They saw me and quickly came in my direction.

"Caleb!" Caroline exclaimed with a smile. "Edgar and I are so excited for our youngling gathering this Wednesday. Edgar even wants to get involved with our leadership team. Please consider it. He's such an amazing young man and just loves the Great King and the Scroll."

I didn't know what to say. I just nodded my head and tried to smile as best I could. Joseph was nowhere to be seen but that was normal being that it was King's Day. Many others were gathered around us, speaking, laughing, and socializing with one another. Eric, the assigner of abilities, had a group of people circled about him. He seemed to be showing them a new banner which must have just been hung, for I did not recognize it. It read, *'The Castle of the Great King: A Place Where Warriors Are Made.'*

"And that is what we do here," Eric was proclaiming with much pride. "We make warriors. This is the vision of our Captain David. We are only 250 members away from reaching our goal of 1,000 every King's Day. And as of this past Wednesday, we have eighty younglings attending their weekly meetings. Yes, the Great King would be pleased." Eric then noticed me and said, "Ah! And here is one of our own instructors of our beloved younglings, dear Caleb. He is a mighty warrior indeed. And look!" he continued, motioning toward Caroline and Edgar, "He is continually mentoring these young warriors."

Every eye in the crowd was upon me, and it seemed that they all expected me to say something. What was I to say? My world was turning upside down. Six months earlier, I had gone from being an unbeliever to an ardent Castle attender. But now, that very source of my life, pride, and hope was crumbling. You must understand, it was not the Scroll that was falling apart in my mind but the Castle. It was as if a tiny snowball had been pushed down a hill, and as more and more time went on, the more it grew. At first, I had a few concerns, like seemingly minor discrepancies, but now they expanded to lacking almost all confidence. My view of the Castle was changing. I no longer saw it as I had before, yet, I wasn't able to fully let it go. I couldn't. For, if the Castle was not true, what did that mean of the Scroll?

My mind was racing in every direction, and I was ready for it to land somewhere. But it couldn't, for there were still too many questions left unanswered. As I glanced at the new banner hanging in all its glory and splendor, I was certain of one thing: the Castle was not making warriors. On the contrary, it was making people who called themselves warriors, many of whom could not even wield their weapons.

My gaze now returned to Eric and his circle of companions, with their eyes fixed upon me. I wasn't sure what to say. I dreadfully wanted to just leave, but I felt it would be rude to say nothing.

The words seemed to leap from my mouth. "Have any of you killed a dragon?" I asked simply. All of their expressions changed. "Are we really warriors?" I continued. "Or are we just stage-actors?"

I wish I had said nothing, and so I quickly left the Castle before I offended, confused, or upset anyone else. *Where warriors are made*, I repeated to myself. I am no warrior but I should be. I could be. How hard would it be? I had my sword and my shield. I had faith in the Scroll and the Great King.

I was by now halfway between the Castle and my home. There was the forest, off to the right. I looked at it. Only twice had I ever entered that forest, both times driven back by dragons and fear. But now my fear was gone. I was tired of looking for others to train me. I knew the Scroll, and I knew that the Great King was sovereign and that He was with me.

I turned my gaze upon the forest, and with resolute courage and determination, I made my way thus. I fixed my shield upon my left arm and drew my sword. Nothing would stop me now. I would kill dragons and teach others to do the same. No more games. No more deception and foolishness. No more compromising of the truth to make people feel better. This would be real, true, and effective.

I was only a few paces away from the forest. I thought of my grandparents, who had died by the claws of dragons. That would not be my fate. They trusted in the Castle; I trusted in the Scroll. I shouted a war cry and ran within the forest, ready to meet my enemy. All was still. I shouted aloud, "Caleb, warrior of the Great King is here! Come, dragons! Come and fight me!" I continued to walk deeper and deeper within the woods. There was no going back now. Darkness seemed to be creeping in around me at every side.

I wasn't sure of which way I had come from, and it seemed like I might not be able to find my way out, with or without a dragon's head. Fear began to enter my heart. What in the world was I doing? Even Captain David, a great soldier of the Great King, wouldn't enter the forest by himself! I then started walking backwards, quietly, hoping to soon exit the forest. My breathing was the one thing I couldn't seem to silence, and it seemed like my breath echoed throughout the woodland.

Then I heard the one sound I feared most. It was a low, low gurgling noise, deep and loud. It seemed to shake the ground. I looked to my left, and there, only about thirty paces or so away, was an enormous dragon, crouched like a lion. Its head, all by itself, seemed the size of a large ox. The head that Captain David had held up, only a week earlier, was like nothing compared to this.

I turned toward the dragon, feeling I could faint at any moment. It was as red as blood, and its eyes were as yellow as the sun. It looked at me with a seeming delight, as if it could sense my inadequacy. I wanted to run. With all my heart I wanted to flee, but I knew that running from a dragon was the worst idea in dragon fighting, for the enemy would no doubt bite or grab me from behind or breathe fire upon me and burn me to a crisp.

I barely found enough strength to raise up my shield and hold up my sword with my arms shaking. My courage was all but gone, and yet, I had a small hint of faith remaining. Even though my words were spoken through shaking lips I addressed my enemy, "I am a servant of the Great King! You will not triumph!" The dragon laughed in response, a sound which I cannot describe and never want to remember. But its effect was what it desired. I began to lower my sword and lose all hope. The dragon then stood up to its full height and towered over me. I dropped my sword. My shield, however, stayed between me and the enemy, as I slowly continued to step backwards.

My foe, however, was done with games. In a fierce and quick anger, it struck me. The blow sent me flying nearly twenty feet through the air and I landed upon my back. I'm certain if it wasn't for my shield, I wouldn't have survived that first attack. I was now paralyzed, as the wind was knocked out of me. The dragon strode to where I was, his massive head and fierce teeth directly over me. He raised his head for the killing stroke. I wondered, in that last moment, where I had gone wrong. Were the Scroll and the Great King even real? Had I just believed a false religion? In despair, I was now going to die.

But just as the great beast began to descend upon me, a cloaked figure ran to my side and scooped me up with such speed as I had never seen before. The dragon's sharp teeth just missed me by a fraction of an inch. I landed at the base of a giant tree and looked to behold a figure in a black cloak, armed with a sword, between me and the dragon, but his back was to me.

"This one will not fall into your hands," he declared to the beast. "Not today."

He spoke as calmly as one would speak to his own child. The dragon raised up its long neck for another killing stroke, but as it descended upon my rescuer, he dashed to one side as quick as lightning, swung his sword with a force I had never before witnessed, and severed the dragon's head from its body. The gigantic carcass fell to the ground with a crash.

The man then turned to me, and right away I recognized him. He was the old, bearded man I had often seen within the forest.

Chapter 16

The man just looked at me, still holding his sword, covered in the black blood of the dragon. It was the first time I had seen his face up close. His eyes were like windows into a vault of wisdom and knowledge. He slowly lowered his sword.

"You shouldn't be here," he said calmly.

"Forgive me," I said. "And thank you. You no doubt saved my life."

"Think nothing of it," he replied, somehow being kind while not smiling. "Let me now show you the way out, and be sure to never come back. Providence has arranged your rescue today, but it may not be so next time."

"Wait," I said, confused and frustrated at the fact that I was delaying our departure and therefore keeping us within such a deadly forest. "How did you do that? I mean, who taught you how to kill a dragon?"

"That is a good question, but it requires a long and somewhat complicated answer," he replied. "The simple answer is this: I trained. And I trained with others of a like mind. And we were taught by others who had gone before us, though mainly by the Scroll itself."

"Can you teach me?" I asked, for the very spectacle I had witnessed had gripped me. And as this man had chopped the head off of the dragon, I felt like he also severed all of my frustration and even some of my confusion. He was, so it seemed, what I wanted to be.

"Can I teach you?" he replied. "To be honest, probably not. For you cannot truly learn the ways of the Great King until you are fully devoted to Him. I know you, boy. I've seen you entering the Castle. Why don't you let them train you?"

"I have," I testified. "And they have trained me as well as they can. I did learn some good things there, though it came in a package with many wrong things. But nevertheless, I am at the end of my rope. And I am willing to be fully devoted to the Great King."

"At the end of your rope, eh?" the man asked. "That's good. For that is where the Great King waits for those who will enter into true Kingdom activity. Still, it isn't enough. I'm sorry but I can't train you. It will be too hard. You won't stick with it and will therefore waste both our time. Believe it or not, you are only about fifty paces from the edge of the forest," he said pointing behind me. "Hurry now before more dragons come. Farewell."

He then turned and began to walk deeper within the forest.

"Wait!" I called out. "Where are you going?"

"That is not your business," he said.

"Please!" I cried out again, as the cloaked man began to disappear deeper into the woodland. "Please tell me where you are going!"

I heard the man faintly laugh. "I'm going deeper within the forest, but that is no place for you."

My heart was racing. There I was, in the midst of an evil forest. To one side of me, lay a dead dragon which was nearly my death. Behind me, as I looked over my shoulder, I could barely see the green open grass country which represented safety and comfort. And yet before me, a man had now disappeared deeper into the forest—a man who had what I wanted. *Get out of here you fool*, I told myself.

But I couldn't. I knew that with all my heart I wanted what I had just witnessed. I wanted to be a skilled warrior of the Great King. What I beheld from this stranger, who people had labelled a *backslider* and a *rebel,* was more skill and wisdom than any other I knew. I was still trembling with fear, and my body wanted to leave, but my spirit wanted to follow the stranger. It was as if something within me was saying, *Follow him! Now!*

But another part of me was saying, *If you go after that man, you will be criticized by everyone you love and hold dear.* And yet, even in my limited knowledge of the Scroll, I knew that it warned against the fear of man. All that mattered is what the Great King thinks. I knew that I had delayed too long, and the stranger was already far, far ahead of me. It didn't matter. The voice within me had overcome the selfish desires of my flesh.

I rose to my feet, retrieved my sword, and quickly ran in the direction I had last seen the stranger. I considered calling out to him, but this was dragon territory, so I decided it was better to be quiet. I kept running, praying and hoping that the man was going in a straight line; otherwise, I would be lost for sure.

Just when I had begun to lose hope, I thought I saw him, far ahead, but his black cloak disappeared once more. I continued my pursuit, though I was about to collapse from exhaustion. Just when I thought I could go no further, I thought I saw an opening ahead. *It must be another exit out of the forest,* I thought. But this was unlikely, for the forest was said to be unmeasurable. Then I saw it for sure. It was true. The forest ceased. Overjoyed at the sight, I ran out from the dense woodland without hesitation. What I saw was astonishing.

I had not exited the forest but had instead entered an open field within the forest, about half a mile across with a few homes scattered throughout it. The total people I saw were approximately fifty men, women, and children. They were all armed with bows and swords and seemed to be training. In the middle of the open oasis was a fire, and there was a deer roasting over it, while a few women seemed to be preparing a meal of some kind. And there, directly before me, was the man in the black cloak. He was grinning slightly, though still carried a sober expression on his face.

"So," he said. "You chose to follow me deeper into the forest instead of return to the comforts of the world. Perhaps, maybe, you are ready to train after all."

"What is this place?" I asked him in amazement.

"Follow me," the man said.

I came alongside him, and we walked together. As we came closer, I was able to take in more of what was happening. Off to our left, a group of women was practicing archery. A few things I noticed right away. First of all, only women seemed to wield the bow; this I now understood, for I had read it in the Scroll. Secondly, there were three aged women, who seemed to be leading them in their archery. The older women were assisting some of the ladies in their skill, instructing when to shoot and when to retrieve arrows. Lastly, I noticed that it wasn't only adult women, but younger ladies and even girls, maybe about five or six years of age.

I now turned my attention to the other side of the field. The men were there, all holding both sword and shield. Just as with the women, so it was with the men. There were a few men, all more aged than the rest, walking amongst them and giving instruction. And there were also children, some only seven or eight years old. The men seemed to be doing drills; this particular one was how to parry a mighty blow of a dragon. One warrior would take his shield, simulating a dragon, and bring it down full force upon the other who would parry, or countermove, with his shield and then simulate a striking blow.

Something else intriguing was how everyone within this hidden oasis seemed to be more—how would you say it—more their gender. What I mean is this: the women seemed extremely feminine and the men extremely masculine. I had obviously known many females in my first twenty years, but these women were different, not only in the way they looked, with their long hair flowing in the gentle breeze and their long garment wrapping them in modesty, but also in the way they conducted themselves. I was immediately drawn to it, in a holy way mind you, as one is drawn to a sunset, when the bright fading colors of the day reflect off the gentle horizon.

In the same way, I noticed that the men were extremely masculine. They were strong and serious. I sensed that they were a band of brothers, devoted to each other completely. They looked like men, carried themselves as men, and behaved as men, in a way that made me feel quite conscious-stricken. One of the men approached me and the aged man who I had followed.

"Captain Samuel," he said with much respect, "our exercises are almost finished. Should I call everyone together for our feast?"

"Do as you see best, dear Stephen," my accomplice replied. "I trust your judgment."

"Captain?" I repeated as I looked at the man. "You are the captain of these warriors?"

The man smiled. "I am not *the* captain. I am one of many captains."

"More than one captain?" I asked. "How many captains are there?"

Captain Samuel then lifted his voice, and it echoed through the hollow. "All captains, come to me!"

Immediately, many men, around ten, ran and presented themselves to Captain Samuel. "Look before you, my boy," he said to me. "All of these men are captains. Every husband and father is a captain, for so it says in the Scroll. Three of us are captains of captains; nevertheless, all of these men have the authority and responsibility to lead their wives and children. They are also to minister to the army of the Great King."

I looked upon all the men with a sense of amazement mixed with fear. I then noticed Nathan, the man I had met at the slaying, standing there with a smile on his face.

"This young man," Captain Samuel said to his men, "is Caleb. And he is our guest today."

"How did you know my name?" I asked with surprise.

"I know much about you, Caleb," he replied. "But that is a conversation for another time. Come! Let us feast together and enjoy each other's love and fellowship."

Many of the captains came and shook my hand. Their love and sincerity were overwhelming, and though it reminded me of the same treatment I had received at the Castle, something was different; it was more real. Captain Samuel introduced me to the two other captains of captains. Their names were Benjamin and Enoch. I could tell that I had just walked in on the end of a very hard and arduous training session. But it was something that these warriors seemed to rejoice in.

We all ate together, and I beheld the way the husbands and wives served each other. I also noticed how the children stayed close to their parents and were, for the most part, free from all folly. I was touched to the heart at how they loved their parents through their respectful actions. I also beheld both married and unmarried ladies, being kind to me, and yet, they did not act like other women I knew. Their behavior was just as modest, pure, and beautiful as their outward appearance.

"So," Captain Samuel said, as he came and sat beside me. "What do you think about all you see here?"

"I can't believe it," I said honestly. "It's wonderful."

The man nodded his head. "By the grace of the Great King, it has been quite incredible. But it is so because of hard work, devotion to the Great King, and devotion to each other. Such devotion is difficult because it requires forfeiting the devotions of this world, but in the end, it is well worth it."

"Why have I never heard of this place?" I asked, but then asked another question before he could answer. "Actually, why doesn't the entire Castle know of this place? I know many people who would love to see this."

Captain Samuel's expression changed a bit. "You might think so, Caleb. But you must understand that there is often an enormous difference between what people say they want and what they actually want. For example, you think there are many people in the Castle who would like this. I don't disagree with you that they would like the idea of it. But when they counted the cost, it would be too much for many of them, for they would have to give up much of what they hold dear."

"I don't understand," I said. "What would they have to give up? Only a few hours every King's Day, right?"

Captain Samuel shook his head. "Oh no, my boy. We do this multiple times a week, and not only that, the individual families that make up this army train every day in their own homes."

"You train every day?" I repeated with shock. A part of me was disappointed by this; another part of me was thrilled with the idea.

"Well," continued the elder, "it depends on what you want to accomplish. If you want to hold a sword and shield, know some head knowledge about the Scroll, such as formations and such, then all you need to do is *train* one day a week." Then his countenance grew fierce, but quiet. "But if you want to kill dragons, then you must train daily. The army of the Great King must be your life."

Captain Benjamin, who had also joined us, explained further. "For this reason," he stated, "many of your acquaintances at the Castle will not become truly proficient warriors. They aren't willing to sacrifice what it takes. They don't want to give up, for example, going to the games many nights a week. They go there to be entertained, and in doing so, forfeit the time necessary to truly train as they are called to do."

"Not only do they lose precious time," inserted Captain Samuel, "but they often lose the hearts of their children as well, to the point that the children doubt the very words of the Scroll itself. They allow their children to go to the plays that the traveling theater promotes, and in doing so, they lose their children to the philosophies of this world."

I had not yet been to a play of the traveling theater in my short time back in Ravenhill, but I knew many in the Castle that went as often as possible. There was even talk about building a permanent theater in the village.

"This is why we do this," Captain Samuel continued, "for the most part, in secret. If we opened up this training ground to all people, regardless of where their true devotion lay, then we would end up with what you see in the Castles. We would end up with quantity but not quality. By contrast, the Great King, when He walked this earth, was focused upon quality, even to the point of turning those away who may have had a level of sincerity, but who weren't willing to give up everything for His cause."

I was amazed at what I was hearing. It was incredible. One thing that made an immediate impression on me as I sat was how Captain Samuel had tried to talk me out of training. He had told me when he saved me from the dragon that it would be too hard. I compared this to the attitude of the Castle and realized they were completely contrary to each other. The Castle's priority was trying to get people to be part of their group, despite the condition of their resolve. These people, these rebels, weren't interested in numbers. They had tried to talk me out of joining them. They wanted true devotion. It actually reminded me of how the Great King called for soldiers when He had walked on the earth.

Things were beginning to make sense, at least, more than before. It was, however, so much to take in at once that I needed further explanation.

"You said that the theater promoted the thinking of the world," I said. "I've never heard that before."

93

"Let me give you an example," Captain Benjamin explained. "Have you noticed that in the Castle both men and women wield the sword and bow?"

"Yes," I said, "though in the Scroll, it forbids such practice. It says that men wield the sword and women wield the bow."

"Exactly," Captain Benjamin said. "Well, I am now nearly seventy years old. Many years ago when I was a child attending the Castle, only men wielded the sword and only women wielded the bow."

"Really?" I said amazed and confused. "What changed?"

"The culture changed," he answered. "And the Castle conformed to the world. But this is my point, young man. It was the theater that brought about the transition. They started doing plays which depicted men wielding bows and women wielding swords. Every time people sat in front of those plays, they were viewing the false advertising of the enemy—which was chipping away at their resolves to stay true to the Scroll. And so, the people of the Great King were being defeated from the inside out, in the name of entertainment."

"That's unbelievable," I said. "Why haven't I learned this at the Castle?"

"Because they are, to some extent, blind to what is really going on," Captain Samuel said. "Many of them think they are following the Great King and the Scroll, when in fact they are following a *great king* that they have invented in their minds. A *great king*, for example, who changes his scroll to accommodate progressive ideas of culture."

"This is the great trickery of the enemy," Captain Benjamin said. "The enemy defeats the people in the Castle, without them even knowing it. The greatest weapon of the enemy is deceit. And when someone is being deceived, by definition, they don't know it."

I sat there in a fog of confusion, amazement, sadness, and frustration. I had come out of the evil webs of the world, only to find myself entangled in another web of man's religion. Somehow, and to my surprise, I understood the words of these men. It was as if my heart had been prepared to hear the truth.

"Enough talk," Captain Samuel said as I sat, deep in thought. "Pick up your sword. It's time for your first lesson."

Chapter 17

By this time, I could faintly see the last glows of dusk hanging on to the western sky. Most of the families had departed or were just leaving. All that remained were Captain Samuel, Nathan and his family, and me, for Captain Benjamin had also left for his home. I would later find out that most of the families lived in the village, while mainly Captain Samuel, and at times a few others, lived in the Oasis. The bonfire was now our source of light. Nathan's wife, Leah, along with his two sons and one younger daughter, sat along the side of the fire watching us. Nathan stood beside Captain Samuel, both men holding their swords. I, a supposed warrior of the Great King, stood there holding my sword, and yet, having no idea at all what to do with it.

"Before you learn how to engage a dragon, you must simply learn how to wield your sword," Captain Samuel said. "The best way is simple combat with other warriors."

Nathan then stepped forward. "Your sword is an extension of not only your body but also your soul," he said. "If you are fearful, your sword will be dull and without effect. If your heart is courageous, your sword will be sharp enough to cut through any dragon's scale."

"In the same way," added Captain Samuel, "if your mind is clouded, your stroke will be slow. And yet if your mind is alert and at peace, your sword will be faster than a bird's wing. Now, close your eyes."

I obeyed this man's instruction, a man who only six hours earlier was someone I regarded as a rebel and my enemy. For whatever reason, I now trusted him. In a way, he reminded me of William. With my eyes closed, all was pitch black. I could feel the heat of the fire upon my face, and I could hear the crackles of the burning cedar. I sensed that Nathan and Captain Samuel were slowly walking around me.

"You must be free from fear," Captain Samuel said. "The knowledge in your head is important, but if you don't believe it in your heart, it counts for nothing. You must trust in the Great King. You must trust in His providence. You must not fear. Don't move...."

All was quiet. For whatever reason, I felt like I was able to apply the instruction. I wasn't afraid. I knew that the Great King was with me. I then heard a slash in the air and the breeze of a sword stroke passing just in front of my face.

"Your heart is prepared for this, my son," Captain Samuel said, as he, and I guessed also Nathan, continued to walk around me.

"Lift your sword in front of you," he said.

I obeyed. I then felt light clanks of steel on steel as they gently began tapping their swords against mine. The taps became stronger.

"Never allow your sword to fall from your hands," Nathan said. "But even more importantly, never let it fall from your mind and your heart. Your sword is the embodiment of the Scroll. When you wield it, you put forth the truth and power of the Scroll. It is the words of the Great King, His truth, and His person which cuts into the dragon, not the steel."

As Nathan spoke, something changed within me. At the thought of my sword being the embodiment of the Scroll, I suddenly saw things differently. It wasn't me, alone, in the forest fighting dragons. The Great King was standing in the gap, between me and my opponent.

"Open your eyes," commanded Captain Samuel. He stood before me with his sword raised. I sensed that Nathan was behind me.

"I'm going to swing my sword down upon you," he said. "I won't do it at full force. I want you to lift your sword and block it. Are you ready?"

I nodded with some apprehension, for I had never done such things. The sword came down. I raised my sword to block it. A loud clang echoed for a second in the clearing.

"That was good," he said. "This time, do it without any fear or reserve, and afterward, swing your sword at me. Don't worry. I can see the trepidation in your eyes. You won't hurt me. You need to get accustomed to your sword. Get ready."

I readied myself. His sword came down. I blocked as I did before, this time with more confidence and countered with more bravery than I would have guessed possible. He quickly dodged my blow.

"Very good," he said with a smile. "This time, do the same thing, then turn around quickly and engage Nathan. He will come at you first and then you must counter."

This went on deep into the night. I can still remember that first training session: Nathan and Captain Samuel patiently instructing me in the ways of the sword. The sparks of the fire rising into the sky, with the stars overhead. Leah and her children, all asleep on the ground with the exception of her eldest son, Levi, who watched us with enthusiasm.

"Well done," said Captain Samuel finally. "It is late."

"Thank you," I said, not knowing really what to say.

"You are welcome," Captain Samuel replied.

"Well, is he one of us now?" asked Nathan.

Captain Samuel paused. "That remains to be seen. Obviously, he can't be a true soldier of the Great King unless he is all in."

"I want to be all in," I said in complete sincerity. "I will train with all my heart and soul, just as the Scroll says."

"Yes," agreed Nathan. "Always follow the Scroll."

"We shall see," said Captain Samuel. "Come back tomorrow, around mid-afternoon. For tomorrow, we will begin training you in the arts of the shield. Oh, and one more thing; don't tell anyone about this place."

"Yes, sir," I replied.

"I will walk him home," said Nathan.

We then entered the forest upon a trail which Nathan assured me was always free from dragons, though I noticed he still walked with both sword and shield in hand while I held the lantern.

"There is something special about you," Nathan said as we walked along.

"What do you mean?" I asked.

"Well," he began. "First of all, you are naturally gifted with the sword. You will quickly become proficient."

"And secondly?" I asked, sensing that he was holding back his words.

"Captain Samuel has never done that before," he said. "What I mean is, he has never trained someone who he had just met. Usually people have to earn that right. They have to be fully trustworthy. Don't misunderstand me; I'm glad that he accepted you so quickly. I liked you from our first real conversation in the marketplace that day. I'm just curious what it is about you that made him instantly accept you and teach you. He even referred to you as *son*. You are blessed."

"What does someone usually have to do to get trained by him?" I asked curiously.

"It basically comes down to what they really believe," he explained. "If they aren't going to take the Scroll and training seriously, then they will not only waste his time, but they will bring down the army. They have to be all in. They have to be willing to change anything based on the Scroll. The way they see everything must be seen through the Scroll. I'm not yet sure if that describes you. I hope it does. But somehow you've seemingly convinced Captain Samuel that it is so."

We now came to the end of the trail, though, oddly enough, we were still in the forest. Nathan stopped.

"Where's the opening?" I asked.

"About one hundred feet that way," he said, pointing forward with his sword.

"Are we going then?" I asked.

He smiled. "Not *we*, but *you*. I return to my wife and children. But you must give me the lantern."

"But how will I see?" I asked.

"The sword," he answered gently. "Hold it out in front of you and walk. Remember, the sword is the Scroll. It will illuminate your steps."

I looked within the pitch black forest before me, hoping to see the fields at the far side. There was only darkness. I looked back at Nathan. "Seriously?" was all I could say.

He laughed. "It's late, my friend," he said as he headed back up the trail. "Trust in the Scroll," was the last thing I heard him say before I saw the last glimmer of his lantern disappear.

Then all was completely dark.

Chapter 18

There I was, in the middle of the forest in the middle of the night. It was pitch black. At the time, I felt that Nathan had gone a little too far regarding my training. If I strayed from the path in the wrong direction, I would be killed by a dragon. I decided to take Nathan's words to heart. I held my sword out in front of me, though I couldn't see it, and I prayed I was facing in the direction that would lead me to the prairies that surrounded the forest. I took a deep breath and began to walk.

I could hear the crunch of leaves and sticks under my feet, clearly revealing that I had left the end of the path behind me. I only hoped I wouldn't go the wrong way or that I wouldn't bump into a sleeping dragon! I continued walking, slowly but surely, and had taken about twenty paces when something happened.

Something was glowing in front of me. I immediately guessed that it was moonlight, shining down upon me, and that I had therefore made it into the prairies. But as my eyes adjusted, I was astonished. It was my sword! The glow was faint but clear, and it seemed to illuminate my steps and only my steps. I couldn't use it to see far in front of me, which was a frustration at first. But then I noticed that the sword would slightly pull one direction or the other as if it was guiding me.

And in this way the sword led me on and gave me just enough light to be sure of my next step. Soon I was outside of the forest, upon the gentle grasslands, with the moon lighting the sky about me.

What was that? I wondered.

It was the Scroll, a voice within me replied. *The sword is the Scroll, and the Scroll gives you both direction and the light you need.* I hurried home, fearful that I would soon wake up, and that all I had experienced was just a dream.

I woke about midmorning and quickly went to the market. The previous night had not been a dream. I had found people who would teach me the art of dragon warfare, and I was excited to continue my training in the Oasis.

Mondays were always busy, and I needed to get a head start on the new week, especially if I was going to train daily. I was surprised to find Justin waiting for me.

"Are you alright?" he asked sincerely.

"Of course," I replied. "Why do you ask?"

"Eric told me that you weren't yourself yesterday. He said you seemed very upset and criticized the new banner they were putting up in the Castle."

I remembered that look on the people's faces as I accused them of putting on a show.

"I was a little frustrated," I confessed. "But it's better now."

"What are you frustrated about?" Justin asked. "It seems that you are changing and not for the better. I'm afraid you're backsliding or falling away. Do you still believe in the Scroll and the Castle?"

"Of course," I assured him. "It's just...I have questions."

"Well," he explained, "questions are fine. But don't forget how much the Castle has done for you. You've become a soldier of the Great King, and it's all due to the Castle and the leadership of Captain David. You are here, with a home of your own and with good friends, all because of the help of the Castle."

I didn't know what to say. Despite the amazing experience I had the night before, I still felt conflicted. My heart still greatly loved the Castle and Captain David, as well as the experiences I had there. For a second, I wondered if I was being led astray by Nathan and Samuel, but I quickly dismissed the idea.

"I am fine, my friend," I assured Justin. "And I am thankful for the Castle and Captain David, and especially, your friendship. Please be patient with me. I'm just working through some things."

Justin took a deep breath and smiled. "You know I will, brother."

After work that day, I quickly took hold of my weapons and went to the edge of the forest at the same place I had exited the previous night. I wasn't sure whether to enter on my own or wait. Just as I was about to enter the forest and look for the path, Nathan found me. He showed me the path and we walked together to the meeting.

I beheld a similar scene from the day before. Men and women, along with their children, were training for battle against the enemy. As we walked calmly past the line of female archers, one of them turned and looked my way. I didn't recognize her from the day before. I was sure she hadn't been there, for I would have remembered her. There was a beauty in her person and countenance that took my breath away. Her glance was for only a second, but her eyes possessed a depth that threatened to capture my heart for a lifetime.

"Who is that woman?" I asked Nathan.

He followed my gaze. "That is Elizabeth. She has been with us since she was young. And no, she isn't yet spoken for."

I quickly glanced over and saw that Nathan was smiling.

We now approached the men of the camp. Captain Samuel greeted me with a gentle and sincere warmth.

"Welcome back, Caleb. I hope you are rested, for we have much to do."

I soon found myself standing alongside twelve other men. Both Captain Samuel and Captain Benjamin stood before us.

"Today we focus upon the shield," Captain Samuel began. "Remember what the Scroll says: *The shield represents your confidence in the Great King.* When you stand before a dragon, always begin by keeping your shield between you and the enemy."

Captain Samuel then looked at me with sunken eyebrows.

"What is your shield made of?" he asked kindly.

"It is iron," I replied. I then looked to those around me and noticed that their shields were made of wood. I felt I needed to justify myself. "I'm not sure if you know," I said respectfully. "But they've recently discovered, through much research, that iron is the most protective element against dragon fire."

"So I've heard," Captain Samuel replied. He then motioned to Nathan's son, Levi, who quickly ran to a nearby storehouse and returned with a wooden shield.

"Here," he said as he handed me the shield and took mine away.

I obeyed, though with some confusion. We then continued.

"If you stand behind your shield with fear and doubt," continued Captain Samuel, "it will not block the flames of your opponent. You must instead stand behind your shield with courage, confidence, and an attitude of victory. It isn't the shield that protects you but the power of the Great King!"

We then did drills which involved blocking sword blows with our shields. From time to time, I would look over at the ladies who were doing their archery training. My eyes fixed upon Elizabeth. Her long, red hair was blowing in the gentle breeze. And as she slowly pulled the arrow back to her cheek, the look in her eyes was both fierce and beautiful to behold. I was suddenly reminded of the cloaked figure I had seen in the forest, the night the baby dragon was slain.

"Caleb."

It was Captain Benjamin.

"Pay attention, my son," he said with a smile.

After our training, we broke bread together. The satisfaction I felt was incredible. There I was, with my brothers and sisters, celebrating together the Great King and His Kingdom. We had trained together, really trained. This wasn't a religious act; it was real devotion. I looked around at all the wonderful fellowship and love. Everyone was together and loved each other. I then noticed a few of the children playing marbles in the dirt by the fire. Nathan sat beside me.

"The children of this army play marbles?" I asked.

"From time to time," Nathan replied.

"What league are they with?" I asked. "The village league?"

Nathan shook his head. "League? Absolutely not. We would be very slow to allow them to play marbles with a league."

I found this to be a fascinating topic. "Why is that?" I asked.

"Because they are only games," Nathan replied with a smile. "Why in the world would we have our children play marbles, checkers, or any other game on a league? That would require time we don't have to give."

"But most of the Castle children do that," I said. "They practice daily."

"Exactly," he replied. "And look at them. The girls can't shoot an arrow straight and the boys don't even know how to hold a sword. They train more for worldly games than they do the battle of the Great King. I fear for them. It's a scheme of the enemy."

Nathan's words reflected my own thinking, months earlier, when I confronted Paul about his son missing the Castle meetings to play marbles. Even back then I thought that it was foolishness, but now my thinking was confirmed. Nathan, however, added something to the conversation which I hadn't considered; these games were somehow a scheme of the enemy.

"What do you mean?" I asked. "Are the games evil?"

"Not at all," Nathan replied. "For you see that my children play them even now. But the focus is wrong. This is a trick of the enemy: to keep us busy with things that are considered good so we forsake the most important things. In this case, they are blind to the fact that revolving their lives around marbles and checkers is likely a waste of time, and they are being robbed of the will of the Great King. You cannot train for the things of the Great King and the things of the world at this same time. You must choose only one to be your focus. The enemy wants you to think you can be devoted to many things at the same time. By definition, to be devoted is to be singular in your attention. I have seen many families fall short of their potential by such schemes of the enemy. Remember, Caleb, following the Great King and being a family of the Scroll is a full-time devotion. There isn't much room for anything else."

Nathan's words pierced my soul, for they seemed to explain why many families I had known weren't experiencing true victory. It wasn't that they were engaging in evil activity, but simply that they were filling their time with things which were temporary and not important in the cause of the Great King.

I then remembered the embarrassing issue with the shield that happened during the training that day. "Why did you take away my shield of iron? It is metal. All of your shields are wood. Wood burns and metal doesn't."

Nathan smiled. He turned and motioned to Levi, who brought him a copy of the Scroll.

"Look here," he said as he opened the Scroll. "Read."

I followed his finger. And this is what I read: *Hold fast to your shield, for with it you will deter all of the fires of the dragon. Make your shield from the willow tree, and season it before use.*

"Make your shield from the willow tree?" I repeated. "It says that in the Scroll?"

"You just read it," Nathan observed with a grin.

"But," I began, bewildered, "if that's what it says in the Scroll, then why in the world doesn't the Castle follow it?"

I then heard Captain Enoch's voice behind me. "Because they trust in their own thinking more than they do the Scroll." He then sat down beside us, his aged eyes piercing into my soul. "This is one of the most important issues regarding your success as a soldier of the Great King. Are you going to trust in the words of men or in the words of the Scroll?"

"But what about the research?" I asked. "They've proven that a steel shield holds up better than a wooden shield."

"It matters not," Captain Enoch replied. "All that matters are the words of the Scroll. There is always some *expert* out there who thinks he knows better than the Scroll does. It all comes back to what you believe about the Great King. Did He get it right, in the beginning, when He first penned this Scroll? Or does He need our help to make the Scroll better?"

"I'm convinced He knows best," I replied.

"Then follow His teaching," Captain Enoch said. "Trust in Him. It just so happens, by the way, that in a real fight, against a real dragon, that a steel shield will heat up to such a degree that it is nearly impossible to hold. And yet a willow shield will not only stand up to the match but will stay very cool." He then looked at the willow shield that Nathan had supplied me, which was next to me. "Consider it a gift," he said. "And use it well. For in the day of combat, you will want to be sure that everything you do is exactly as the Great King has commanded. Otherwise, you will fail."

"Thank you," I said graciously.

Captain Samuel now joined us.

I suddenly remembered the experience I had in the forest, when I tried to save the young girl from the dragon.

"Captain Samuel," I said. "I have a question for you."

"Yes?" he replied.

"Two weeks ago, there was a dragon who was trying to eat a young girl. I went into the forest to save her but was unable. Someone severed the dragon's head from its body but was never seen or heard from. Was that you?"

"No," replied Captain Samuel. "I didn't do it; they did," he said pointing at those around him. "I was out on other business. Some of the other captains heard about it and hurried to the aid of the girl. I think about twenty of our number engaged that dragon. Very rarely will one ever face a dragon alone, and indeed, it should never really happen—not a good idea."

"Why didn't they tell anyone that they did it?" I asked.

"A good question," he replied with a smile. "But for another time. We have more training to do."

The elderly sage then rose to his feet and spoke aloud to all those present. "All husbands and wives on the field. All others sit and watch."

I quickly noticed that those of us watching formed a small circle of men and another of women. The young men and women didn't sit together but separate. A young man, about my age, named Philip sat next to me. I quietly asked him why the single men and women didn't sit together. He looked at me with surprise in his eyes.

"Because we aren't yet married," he replied.

I didn't make the connection, for in the Castle, single men and women often sit together and visit. I turned my attention to the training. What I witnessed on that day, for the first time, was extraordinary. The men formed a half circle around a target which simulated a dragon. Each woman stood directly behind her man.

"Remember," began Captain Enoch, "the two fight as one. You are not two individuals but one fighting unit. The husband, with shield and sword, protects himself and his wife. The wife, with her bow, supports the cause of her shepherd-husband."

The women then shot their arrows at the target, sometimes only missing their husband's head by an inch. The husbands held their shields high and moved together in formation. It was a beautiful sight which I felt I would have never beheld in the Castle.

Afterwards, I spoke with Nathan.

"That was incredible," I said.

"As are all things when done according to the Scroll," he replied. "When husband and wife work together, as the Great King has commanded, they are unstoppable."

"I have a question for you," I continued. "While we were watching you all train, the men and women sat separately. Why?"

"The Scroll speaks of purity and of guarding your heart. We take that very seriously here."

"So then," I replied curiously, "would it be wrong for me to go introduce myself to Elizabeth and visit with her?"

"I wouldn't say it is wrong," he replied kindly. "But depending on how you treated her during that visit, it would definitely discourage her from looking to you as a potential suitor."

"Really?" I said with surprise. "Why?"

"Because, my brother, true women of the Great King are attracted to modesty, respect, and propriety. She knows who you are. You can speak to her, if you feel led to, but be very respectful."

I nodded in understanding. Nathan continued. "Now she is your sister. Do you think you want her to be more?"

"Yes, I do," I boldly replied. "I know that might sound foolish since I don't know her."

"It isn't foolish at all," he replied. "We can know people to a large degree without words. You will get to know her by observation. In the meantime, you must show her who you are by your actions. And if it is the will of the Great King, you must begin to win her heart."

"How?" I asked.

"You show yourself a man of honor and Kingdom discretion."

"Anything else?"

"Yes," he answered. "You show her the courage of a son of the Great King."

"How?" I asked.

Nathan smiled. "You kill dragons."

Chapter 19

The next day was Wednesday. I went to the youngling gathering as usual, though with a different outlook on things. All of the regular younglings were there including Joseph, Edgar, and Caroline. During the opening activity, I pulled Caroline aside.

"I'm worried about you," I said. "I'm worried that you're slipping away."

"What?" she said defensively. "Why are you worried about me? I've never been better."

"I saw you at the forest!" I said in anger, yet keeping my voice as quiet as possible. "I saw you hold the dragon. What were you thinking?!"

Her eyes were filled with surprise, shame, and anger. "Were you the cloaked stranger who shot our dragon?" she asked.

"Our dragon?" I repeated in anger. "No. I wasn't. All I know," I continued, "is that I saw you, Edgar, and Captain David's son conspiring with the enemy."

Caroline smiled maliciously, yet, deep within her eyes, I could still see the girl who wanted to love the Great King. "You need to wake up," she said. "Your expectations are ridiculous. The expectations of the Castle are ridiculous. Everyone does what we were doing the other night. You think I'm walking away from the Great King. You are wrong. I know Him better now than I ever have before."

She then turned to walk away but I beckoned her stay and listen.

"Edgar is poisoning your mind," I told her. "He is bad for you."

Her eyes filled with tears and her expression was terrifying. "Edgar," she said, "is the best thing that ever happened to me. My parents love him. I love him and he loves me. We are one now, Caleb, and no one will ever change that. I know that we will marry."

"But he doesn't even follow the Great King," I said with shock and desperation in my voice.

"Oh please," she said. "Who are you to judge? Edgar loves the Great King well enough. He's here at the youngling gathering, isn't he? What more do you phony Castle-goers want? You claim to be warriors of the Great King. How many dragons have you killed, Caleb? You said it yourself in the Great Hall last King's Day. It's all a joke. But not for me and Edgar. We know the Great King and understand His ways better than any of you do. Now, leave me alone."

She went directly into the arms of Edgar and kissed him. He glared at me, which communicated to leave Caroline alone. I knew at that moment that Caroline had lost her heart; Edgar had stolen it. I wondered what Susanna, the leader of the Youngling Guild, would say. I also feared what Captain David would have to say, seeing that his eldest son was handling dragons.

As I watched the eighty or so younglings there, I wondered where each of their hearts were. I had to believe that some of them were true followers of the Great King. But then again, I had thought the same about Caroline. But that was different—she was led astray by Edgar. What really frustrated me was that her father had some concerns, and it was the Youngling Guild that convinced him to ignore his apprehensions.

Everything was changing for me. I felt like my eyes were opening up to the real state of things; selfishly, I wished I was still blind. I was becoming friends with supposed *rebels* and *backsliders* in the forest. At the same time, I was more and more angering those within the Castle. I didn't know what to do. I acted on sheer impulse. I couldn't help it. I walked out of the meeting and headed to my home.

Ironically, along the way, I bumped into Edgar's father, Simon.

"There you are," he said. "I was coming to find you at the youngling gathering. Did they let out early?"

"No, sir," I replied, trying to hide my inner turmoil. "I just don't feel very well and decided to go home."

"Well, I don't want to keep you long then. I just wanted to extend my thanks for what you've done for my son."

I was shocked. I just stood there, looking at the man, almost to a degree that made him uncomfortable. He continued.

"My son has changed. He is more obedient and respectful to me and his mother. I believe it is the influence of his new lady-friend, Caroline. All of this has actually made me warm up to the Castle. I might even start attending myself."

"That's good," I said, a comment that a week before would have been sincere but now was a source of confusion and concern.

"It's actually shocking, if I'm honest," he explained. "I would have never thought, in all my life, that I would look favorably upon the Castle. I always viewed it as a place of judgment and closed minds. But now, especially through the influence of my son and what he's been learning, I'm seeing that I was mistaken. I see that the Castle is a place of open minds, flexibility, and acceptance. Anyhow, I know you need to get home. Thank you again for all you've done. You were the right man for the job. Good evening."

He then turned and continued on his way, and I on mine. I wanted so badly to talk to him about his son and the baby dragon, but I didn't think it would bother him, just as it was acceptable to Caroline. He said that his son's behavior had improved. I began to piece together in my mind what was actually happening. Edgar had experienced the manipulative power of worldly religion. Instead of being the rebel, he was now the good, Castle-going youngling. He would be respected by all, and yet just as disobedient, in the shadows, as he had ever been.

The next day, I went out to the Oasis. The three captains, Samuel, Benjamin, and Enoch, were sitting together in pleasant fellowship. They greeted me as I approached and invited me to join them.

"What's troubling you, Caleb?" Captain Enoch asked. "You have the cares of the world upon your shoulders."

"Many things are on my mind," I replied. "But first, I have a question. People at the Castle call you rebels and backsliders. They told me you were trying to get me away from the Castle. Is that true?

"Not at all," replied Captain Enoch, his long beard blowing in the gentle breeze. "Our goal for you is the same as the Great King: to slay dragons. If the training of the Castle assists you in that, then praise the Great King. If not, then that's your business. Our battle isn't against the Castle but the Great Dragon. Many warriors at the Castle are true followers of the Great King and we love them dearly. I don't want to fight against them, for they are my brothers. As it says in the Scroll, *Our battle isn't against people, but dragons.*"

Captain Benjamin agreed. "You must never make the people at the Castle, or any people for that matter, your enemy. Some of them are your allies; yet many of them are captives of the Great Dragon. It is your job to love the first and set the latter free. Regarding, however, the claim that we are backsliders and rebels, that is partially true. We do rebel against the popular practices of the Castle which go against the Scroll."

"Something else important to mention," said Captain Samuel, "is that pride can have no place in your heart. It would be easy to compare yourself to them—a very worldly practice indeed—and so feel good about yourself. But it is the Scroll we compare ourselves with, not people."

I sat in thought for a time, and they graciously allowed me the liberty to do so. Their words made sense, as they always did. But then again, so did Captain David's in the beginning. The difference was, however, that their words proved true while many of Captain David's fell empty. I could see the difference in the quality of person and family within these *rebels*. The families that trained weren't perfect, of course, but they were different. They had character. The men were masculine and servant leaders; the women, extremely feminine and powerful homemakers. Their marriages were such as I had never seen. The children were set apart from the world, mature and engaged in the work of the Great King.

"I have another question," I said. "It is regarding the Castle and the Youngling Guild. You don't seem to do things the way they do. They separate their younglings; you keep them together. Why?"

"Good question," said Captain Benjamin. "Simply put, the Scroll doesn't command such a segregation but actually portrays the opposite. The family trains and fights as one unit."

"But how in the world did it come to this?" I asked. "What gave them the idea to separate their children? It seems so foolish."

"Does it really seem foolish to you?" asked Captain Samuel. "Haven't you been serving in such a capacity for some time now?"

"Well, yes. I have been. It seemed normal and good. But now, with my eyes opening up, I see it for what it is."

"So it is with all things," explained Captain Samuel. "It all looks different when you understand the truth. What was wrong is now right, and what was right is now wrong. This is why you must be careful and question everything. Don't take anything for granted. Always consult the Scroll."

"Listen to me," said Captain Enoch. "And I will explain to you how such a detrimental practice became so widely accepted. It began, as most things do, with the practices of the world. The world started, more and more, to separate the children from the parents. For about four decades now, the village schools have become more and more popular.

"This practice, of regularly separating children from parents, led to this present reality that we have a subculture within our society called *youngling*. From the beginning, since the days of the Great King until recently, there was no such word as *youngling*. For all of human history, someone was a small child, and then they quickly transitioned into an adult. But now in our society, there is a new classification of person, that of a *youngling*, which is based off of modern wicked philosophies. And with this new classification is a new expectation. Younglings aren't expected to be responsible and mature soldiers of the Great King but are rather expected to play games and simply *stay out of trouble*.

"The Castle, in conforming to the patterns and ideas of this world, failed to recognize that the world was deterring the maturity of our sons and daughters. The Castle should have resisted. They should have said to the world, *If there is any place that our sons and daughters will not be separated from us, it is here*. But, instead, they conformed.

"So now you have such things as the Youngling Guild. It isn't part of the solution, my friend. It's part of the problem. This is why they try to hire young people, like yourself, to serve in the Youngling Guild. They have so separated their children into a subgroup that the younglings don't really want to be around older people, such as us three, or their parents, but instead they prefer the youngest adults they can find."

"Think about it this way," Captain Samuel added. "If there was such a thing as a Youngling Guild in the Scroll, what kind of men would the Great King want to run it?

Would He want nineteen-year-olds to train up the sons and daughters, or would He want elders to train them up?"

"It would seem to me that He would want the wiser and more experienced," I said. "He would want elders."

"Absolutely," Captain Benjamin agreed. "But here is the good news for you, Caleb. When you are a father someday, and a good father you'll be, you won't be running around looking for someone else to train your children. You will train them. And you will encircle them with older and wiser soldiers to aid you in any way you see fit."

I couldn't contradict or deny any word that the three captains were saying. And the evidence was visible in the attitudes and maturity of their families and children. It was also evident in the Scroll. I realized, once again, how tricked I had been. I had thought to myself, many times before, how the Youngling Guild was such a great thing for parents, and how I, as a parent, would put my children in it as often as I could. Now, everything had changed. Not only would I never put my children in the Youngling Guild, but I wouldn't raise them according to the philosophy of the world which believed that peer-relationships were a necessary part of a child's upbringing. I would be the main companion of my children. And second to me, I would surround them with mature men and women, like Nathan, Samuel, Benjamin, and Enoch. After all, my goal as a parent was to make my children into men and women, not younglings. So instead of surrounding them with children, I would immerse them into the army of the Great King.

Captain Samuel encouraged me. "The questions you are asking are normal and good. You are upon a difficult journey, for not only do you have much to learn, but you also have much to unlearn. Here is a good prayer to pray: *Great King, erase everything I've been told, and erase everything I think I know, and teach me afresh from the Scroll.*"

"Will I ever run out of questions?" I asked.

They smiled and simultaneously answered, "No."

"You never stop learning in the army of the Great King," explained Captain Benjamin. "The moment you stop learning is the moment you start failing."

"Well?" asked Captain Samuel, looking at his fellow captains. "Has this conversation answered our earlier question from this morning? We were just discussing on whether Caleb is ready for the next step. I was concerned that he wasn't and a part of me still is, and yet, I can't help thinking that it is time."

"I agree," said Captain Benjamin.

"It is time," declared Captain Enoch.

"Time for what?" I asked curiously.

Captain Samuel put his hand on my shoulder.

"Time to go dragon hunting," he said.

Chapter 20

We assembled at camp the following morning, just as the dawn began to glow out of the east. The morning mist still clung to the ground as the larks began to welcome the new day. The attitude of everyone, as we gathered, was both kind and serious at the same time. After morning prayer and devotions, we made our way into the thicket with a few mules bearing extra supplies. There were about twenty adults and a dozen children being sent off together. Captain Enoch remained in the Oasis with others while Captain Samuel and Captain Benjamin led the way for us. Nathan was also very involved in the leadership of the hunt, always accompanied by his boys, Levi and Adam. The rest of us were mainly grouped according to families. Despite the time I had spent with the army, I was still inspired and startled at the fact they brought their children along with them. Even young toddlers were strapped upon mothers' and fathers' backs. I had to remind myself that my dismay was due to my experience in the Castle. The Scroll was clear; we do battle together, as families.

I stayed as close to Nathan as possible, for I seemed drawn to him more than any other. He was as a brother to me. We trekked along, quiet and alert. Every man and boy had his sword ready, and every woman likewise readied her bow.

I suddenly had a sense that we were closing in on dragons. I could *feel* it and was surprised that no one else seemed to notice. A low rumble then echoed around us and everyone stopped dead in their tracks. It was the same sound I had heard on the day that Captain Samuel saved my life. I wondered at that moment if anyone ever grew accustomed to such sounds.

"Get ready," Captain Samuel said calmly and only loud enough for us to hear.

All of a sudden, two dragons came upon us from the dense surroundings. They were both like the one I had previously seen a month before—red, walking on four legs, and nearly the size of a small cottage. I raised my shield.

They began spitting fire upon us, though our shields easily deflected them. A volley of arrows then came from the women, and it was fierce. Their precision was perfect. The arrows sank between the scales of the beasts, yet they were far from defeated. Something I noticed—it happened so quickly that I doubted my own vision—was some of the arrows were all aflame, as if the women had lit them before they shot them. At the moment, I dismissed it as my imagination.

The two dragons were now within range to strike upon us, and it seemed to me that they knew who to attack, for they focused upon the strongest and also the weakest of us all. One of them came down upon Captain Benjamin with all its might. The veteran warrior only barely dodged the attack. The other dragon singled me out and swiped quickly with its tail. Those around me had come to my aid but were almost all driven back by this attack.

The dragon then struck at me with its claws, ripping my shield from my grasp, and therefore exposing me fully to its rage. I held my sword now with both hands and prepared to attack. The creature raised upon its hind legs, towering nearly thirty feet in the air, and came down upon me with all its might. At this point, a few things happened all at once that I didn't fully understand until later. Nathan neared within about twenty paces from me and made a motion with his hands in my direction, and before the beast came down upon me, I was pushed by something away from its grasp. Nathan then advanced upon the beast as his wife followed behind her husband with her baby upon her back. She released arrow after arrow, many of which soared only inches away from her husband's head as they went on to meet their mark. The dragon roared in return, infuriated with this turn of events. I looked over to see the other dragon being finished off by many warriors. And as my eyes returned to my own adversary, he was upon the ground lifeless with Nathan and his family standing alert beside him.

Soon all was calm. None of us were injured or lost in the encounter, though my arm was a bit sore from the dragon's attack upon my shield. I looked at the captains as they examined the creatures and made sure all was safe.

"What are they looking for?" I asked Nathan, who sat beside me.

"Many things," he replied. "We must know our enemy. Therefore, we must see if any modifications have been made to their breeding, though in the end, a dragon is a dragon. They also search to make sure that none of the dragons are carrying eggs that will soon hatch."

There was always more to learn. I thought about all that I thought I knew in the Castle. I felt now that I knew almost nothing.

"What did you do?" I asked Nathan, remembering how he came to my aid. "You seemed to push me out of the way, though you weren't beside me. And also, did I see women shooting flaming arrows? How did they light them so quickly?"

"They didn't light them," he replied. "For a few of the women, they only need shoot the arrow and it ignites on its own."

"Ignites on its own?" I replied. "How is that possible?"

"It's their ability," he said plainly. "That is also what I did. I used my ability, which is to move my brethren, for a time, out of harm's way. Do you know about abilities?"

"Yes. I suppose I do. They spoke of it at the Castle."

"And what is your ability?" Nathan asked.

I was hesitant to reply but didn't want to claim no answer. "My ability is working with the Youngling Guild."

Those around me couldn't help but laugh quietly.

My dear friend smiled kindly. "It is good to know how to speak with children. It will help you be a better captain of your own clan one day. But that isn't an ability."

"Well," I said curiously, "how do you discover your ability? Is there a test you take?"

"No test at all," Nathan said. "You discover your ability out here in the forest, as you obey the Great King and as you fight dragons. You'll see. Just give it time, and soon, it will be obvious."

Just then we heard a rumble, not as loud as before, but still strong and near. We grabbed our weapons and spun around.

"There!" someone shouted.

I looked, and there, behind the brush was a dragon. It was aggressive and intimidating but wasn't the same size as the other dragons I had seen. It was smaller, near the size of the dragon that Captain David had slain weeks earlier. But even so, I was still terrified. We all began to approach the beast in a crescent moon formation, but suddenly one of our soldiers called out.

"Wait!" he cried. "Everyone back up!"

His name was Stephen. I looked at Captain Samuel for guidance. He quickly obeyed, backing up slowly, with his shield raised and facing the dragon. Stephen then called for his son, a young man around the age of thirteen.

"Jedidiah!" he shouted. The young man, armed with both sword and shield, came to his side. Everyone there, except for me, knew what was happening. What I then witnessed was unbelievable.

"Are you ready?" Stephen asked his son.

"Yes, Father," was the boy's reply.

Everyone else continued to withdraw except for young Jedidiah.

The dragon seemed to also know what was happening, and I thought for a moment that a wicked smile was upon the creature's face.

Jedidiah pointed his sword outward, toward the dragon. "I challenge you!" he said.

The dragon sprang upon the young man with such force and quickness that I gasped aloud. Jedidiah was knocked to the ground and a small cloud of dust sprang up around him. I couldn't believe what I was seeing! This was too much! I felt I couldn't keep quiet. I started to grip my sword and was just about to attack the dragon when I felt Nathan's hand upon my shoulder.

"Don't even think about it," he said. "This is the young man's fight."

Jedidiah quickly regained his footing. And it seemed to me that he stood stronger and taller than before. He then came at the dragon. For a brief moment, the two opponents exchanged blows as two wild animals within a small den. Yet Jedidiah wasn't out of control. As the battle went on, the dragon seemed to grow more desperate while the boy was surer of himself. Then, as the dragon sprung at the lad, Jedidiah countered with his sword, cutting into the neck of the beast. The dragon thrashed upon the ground a bit, after which the boy, tattered and torn, thrust his sword deep within the heart of the dragon. All of those present let out a shout of celebration, and I felt like I nearly passed out from relief.

Stephen then approached his son, who was standing tall and strong, with both human and dragon blood upon his garments. "Kneel, my son," he said gently. The boy obeyed. And taking his sword, the father knighted his son. "You are no longer a boy but are instead a man. Rise now, a soldier of the Great King."

Jedidiah rose to his feet, and all around applauded and congratulated him. The men shook his hand and so I followed suit. The look on the young man's face was something that fixed in my eyes for many years to come. It was a day of passage for him—passage from childhood to adulthood. Once again, I was amazed. Never in a lifetime would the Castle allow a youngling to fight a dragon amongst an army of six hundred, let alone by himself. And yet it happened. He killed the dragon! It was an achievement that virtually none of my brothers in the Castle had accomplished.

Captain Samuel observed my astonishment. "What do you think of what you've seen?" he asked me.

"It's incredible," was all I could say. "I don't understand how he did it. It all seems impossible."

Captain Samuel smiled. From somewhere behind me, in the mix of all the soldiers, I heard a woman's voice reply to my comment.

"Nothing is impossible when we follow the words of the Scroll," she said.

I didn't see her utter the statement, and yet, I knew who it was. That voice carried within it the gentleness of a butterfly and the strength of a storm. It was beautiful. I turned around and looked. Many were behind me, weaving in and out of friendly conversation, but then I saw her eyes. For only a second, they met mine as she walked away. The eyes of Elizabeth were like a blue, spring mist. I was captivated.

"We will camp here tonight," ordered Captain Samuel. "In the morning, the children and some of their guardians will return. The rest of us continue on."

"Continue?" I said quietly to Nathan. "I thought we were all returning tomorrow."

"No," he replied. "Not this time. We still have a few days ahead of us."

"Why aren't the children coming?" I asked.

"It is too dangerous," he replied.

"I thought all of this was pretty dangerous," I said, half serious and half joking. "What's more dangerous than this?"

"Black dragons," Nathan replied.

As soon as he uttered the words, *black dragons*, my heart seemed to petrify within me. I had not heard any mention of black dragons since my childhood, when Lily and I were lured into the forest by one. I had almost convinced myself, after all of those years, that it was a dream and not real. Nathan noticed the look on my face.

"Are you alright?" he asked.

"Yes," I quickly said, trying to recover myself. "It's just that the Castle never spoke of black dragons."

"The Castle used to know of them," Nathan replied, "long ago, when they still traveled deep within the forest. But today, most are ignorant of them, for they are only seen amongst the mountains."

"Mountains?" I asked. It seemed strange to me that I would have encountered something so rare as a black dragon being just within the forest boundary. Why was the black beast of my childhood so far from its home?

"Yes. The mountains are where they breed," Nathan explained.

"Tell me about them," I said. "What makes them different from the red dragons?" My curiosity bubbled up, for even though I had seen them, it had been in my childhood nearly a decade earlier.

Nathan's countenance was grim. "They are stronger than the red dragons. Their fire is hotter and they have wings and are therefore able to fly. They are crafty and evil."

I was plagued with fear. I had never resolved the question of why that black dragon had tried to lure me to my death so many years earlier. The description that

Nathan gave me, mixed with my encounter as a child, made me want to exit the forest and never return.

"If these dragons are so fierce, evil, and dangerous, then why in the world are we going to where they are?" I asked.

Nathan fixed his gaze upon me. "Because we're going to kill them."

Chapter 21

We arose before sunrise. A quick but hardy breakfast was made, for the day would require much of our strength. I walked over to the fire where the meal was served and began to reach out for the next helping when I noticed another pair of hands reaching out for the same dish. They were the hands of Elizabeth.

"Oh," I said, taken off guard. "Forgive me. Please, ladies first."

Elizabeth smiled. "That is very kind of you, sir, but allow me." And she took the dish and served it to me. "I am honored to serve a warm meal to a brother and fellow warrior," she said.

I was overwhelmed with such words and tried frantically to think of something kind to say in return. There she was, handing me the dish, with arms extended and a beautiful smile on her face. I paused before accepting the meal, for her features— red hair, blue eyes, captivating smile—reminded me of Lily.

"Thank you," I said, receiving the food. "You are a skilled archer. How long have you trained?"

"Since I was young," she replied.

I was trying to remember the words of Nathan; *propriety and respect are to be given*. I motioned to the next dish.

"Please," I said. "Please enjoy your breakfast."

"Thank you," she replied, and she took her meal and went and sat down with some of the sisters.

I was trying to hide the fact that I was breathing heavily. I quickly went and sat down next to Nathan. I was very pleased with the exchange Elizabeth and I had. It was a very modest and respectful conversation, and it only made me more attracted to her than before. I thought that Nathan would have been proud of me.

We ate a quick breakfast and the campfires were extinguished. For the first half of that day, we marched in silence, not seeing any of the enemy. My mind was fixed on many things. I thought about the Castle and all of my experiences there. My mind was tossed back and forth between all the many emotions I felt. I remembered Justin, my first friend in the faith, and wondered if he would ever be with me in the forest killing dragons.

I also thought of all that had happened in the previous weeks at the Oasis. I had met Captain Samuel, trained with him, and was now fighting dragons. Most of all, I thought of Elizabeth. And to be honest, it bothered me. On one hand, I was enamored with her, greatly desiring to speak with her again and win her heart. But on the other hand, who was I? Why would she even consider me as a soulmate? There were many other unwed men in the company. I was the new recruit, fresh from the world and the Castle. I didn't understand the culture of the Kingdom. I hadn't yet read all of the Scroll. I was just fooling myself to think she would consider me.

I didn't want to set myself up for heartache and despair. And yet within me, I heard a voice say, *Are you going to give up that easily?* I sheathed my sword, my left hand still holding my shield, and quickly retrieved my copy of the Scroll. Over the next hour, I glanced at the sacred script, reciting the words in my head. I had decided that I would make myself worthy of this woman I so greatly desired. But then I considered the very words I was reading in the Scroll. They were about the Great King and His plan for all things: *You are His warrior, called to great battles, which the Great King has already prepared in advance for you to do.*

And then it hit me: it's acceptable to try to win Elizabeth, but I didn't need to make her the focus. The focus was the Great King. I would follow Him with all of my heart. And in doing so, if it was His will, I would win Elizabeth. I then realized that I didn't know much about her. I guessed her to be around eighteen years of age, but who were her parents? Every time I saw her, she was with the women, but none of them looked like they were her mother or her sister.

As I drifted back to reality, I noticed the mountains. We were nearing the black dragons. I returned the Scroll to my pouch and readied my sword. I felt fear enter my heart and I knew it was wrong. The Scroll said that fear wasn't ever from the Great King, but I felt that I couldn't help it. Red dragons scared me enough. I couldn't imagine standing my ground before a black dragon. I knew that by the end of the day, I would be able to imagine it well enough.

It was now around noon. Nathan and his wife, Leah, walked beside me. His children had returned home with a woman who would watch over them until their parents returned. I quietly spoke to my dear brother.

"Nathan, where does Elizabeth come from? Who is her family?"

"You ask for the telling of a tragic tale," he replied, "and also a story of redemption and grace."

I waited for some more explanation. Nathan hesitated.

"The telling of someone's story is usually for them to tell," he said. "But it is very appropriate for you to know who her father is, for if you choose to know her more, you must first speak with her father."

This custom wasn't completely foreign to me, for I had heard of it before. Though it had become rare, there were still people who felt it was appropriate. Nathan continued.

"Her father is Captain Samuel."

"Captain Samuel?" I replied. "But he is…"

"So old?" Nathan finished with a chuckle. "I understand your thinking. He adopted her long ago, when she had no one else. That is all part of her story."

Captain Samuel, I thought to myself. *He likes me, though he also knows how much of a novice I am.* I then imagined myself approaching him about pursuing his daughter. It was an intimidating thought.

"How do your people take relationships to the next level?" I asked. "Do they link?"

"Not at all," Nathan said, with much disgust in his eyes at the word *link*. My thoughts of Edgar and Caroline made me understand why.

"I would strongly encourage you," he said, "to never even speak the words *link* or *linking* again. It is the embodiment, in many ways, of the perversion of this world which can look so innocent and yet kill the soul. A healthy relationship, on the other hand, when done according to the Scroll, is pure and right and good. It has the priorities of the Great King as its focus. It isn't a mock marriage as *linking* is, which usually always ends in a mock divorce. It's getting to the marriage altar according to the Scroll, not the way the world does it, which is usually filled with evil and regret."

"What kind of evil?" I asked as we continued on through the forest.

"It's actually very simple," Nathan said. "Would it be alright for you to kiss my wife or hold her hand or spend time alone with her?"

The question made me feel very uncomfortable, even embarrassed and ashamed. "Of course not," I answered.

"Why not?" he asked.

130

"She isn't my wife," I replied. "Those are only things for you to do with her."

"Exactly," he said. "Kissing, holding hands, spending time alone, embracing each other, these are all things intended by the Great King for marriage and marriage alone. What the world calls *linking* is a premature practice of such things. Not only are they inappropriate but almost always the couple doesn't get married. What does that mean they were actually doing?"

His question made perfect sense to me. "It means they were kissing and embracing another person's spouse," I said. I again thought of Edgar and Caroline. I had every reason to believe that they were not going to get married. I had seen it many times before with others. They link for a time, then feelings change, and they break apart. That meant that Edgar was kissing—and doing who knows what—with another man's wife! Soon he would break apart with Caroline, a mock divorce as Nathan said, and her heart would be broken forever. At that moment, I made up my mind that I would do things right with Elizabeth. I just needed to know what to do.

"So, what do I do?" I asked.

"There is more to say at another time," he answered. "But for now, let me say this. You show a woman you are a man of honor by the way you act and speak. You make sure that all of your words and actions are in alignment with the Scroll. You do not simply speak whatever nonsense is in your mind because you want her to hear you speak. Every action and every word must be intentional and meaningful. You must treat her and speak to her as a soldier speaking to his superior's daughter, which she is. However, you must also treat her, as the Scroll says, as a beloved sister with the utmost purity and integrity. If you begin there, you will be on a good start.

"Let me say it again this way," he continued. "In the Scroll, there are only two kinds of relationships between male and female. First, there is that of brother and sister. Secondly, there is that of husband and wife. So, it is actually quite simple. You treat her as your sister until the day that she becomes your wife."

Nathan's words were both helpful and intense at the same time. They were so different from the world, a fact that made me believe they were from the Great King. More and more, I was seeing that there was such a dichotomy between the ways of the world and the ways of the Great King. Interestingly, I didn't feel such a contrast when I attended the Castle.

As I was considering these things, something happened. I felt something. It was so strong that it made me stop dead in my tracks and all thoughts of Elizabeth fled from my thinking. I couldn't restrain my words; they just came out. "Stop!" I said as quietly as I could while still getting everyone's attention.

The company seemed to sense the urgency in my voice and obeyed.

Captain Benjamin quickly came to me. "What is it?" he asked.

I wasn't sure what was happening within me, but I could sense something. It was outside of me. I could even sense where it was. I pointed my sword to the northeast and everyone followed my gaze.

"Something is coming," I said. "I know it." I then felt something else, stronger and larger coming from the opposite direction.

"And that way," I said motioning to the southwest. "Something larger approaches."

All of this happened so quickly that I finally realized all I had said and done. For a fraction of a second, I felt huge amounts of shame and embarrassment and half-expected for everyone to burst out laughing. Something different happened.

"Listen to him!" Captain Samuel declared. "He can discern their coming and going! Quick! Get in formation!"

Within only a few seconds, we were all in formation for a multi-directional conflict. The men were in the outer ring of the circle while the women were within. All were facing outwards.

Then I saw them.

132

It is difficult for me to describe what I felt when I beheld a black dragon for the first time since my childhood. My skin grew cold, and I felt that every heartbeat was laboring. The color of the dragon's skin transcended beyond pitch black. The yellow eyes seemed to pierce through me, as if the dragon could look into my very soul and knew all of my darkest secrets. Both dragons were now in view.

They were much larger than red dragons. Their necks were too wide for one sword stroke to sever. For a second I thought to myself, *What in the world are we doing here? We are all going to die!* Then, somewhere deep within me, I was reminded that to die in obedience to the Great King was the most honorable of all deaths. Though, at the time, this thought comforted me little.

One of the dragons came at us while the other stayed back. All of the sisters let their arrows loose, mainly aiming at its eyes. The dragon let out a roar that shook the ground. The men then advanced. Our swords slashed at the creature, who then spun around, swinging its massive tail upon us. I quickly ducked the blow though many others were hurdled into the surrounding foliage. The dragon then grabbed me with its claws and raised me from the ground. I couldn't breathe under its force and would soon lose consciousness. The dragon raised me in front of its mouth. I could faintly hear Nathan's voice from below.

"Dragon's fire! Dragon's fire!" he shouted.

Everyone cried out in fear. I looked over my shoulder at the company. Ladies were releasing arrows and the men were running toward the dragon with raised swords. Then I noticed Elizabeth. Both her hands were raised towards me, palms open, with tears in her eyes.

I then turned to the dragon, whose hideous face was only a few yards away from me. It opened its mouth. I could see the fire kindled deep within its throat and feel the intense heat. The dragon took a deep breath. The last thing I saw before I closed my eyes were the flames bursting forth towards me.

Chapter 22

I knew at that moment that all was lost. Time seemed to stop so as to allow me one last thought before death. At least I would be remembered as a warrior of the Great King. Perhaps Elizabeth, though we only spoke once to each other, would remember me as a man worthy of her love. Now I was ready. I would die. And yet, I didn't. I felt heat, though mild, all around me and I wasn't burning. I opened my eyes and this is what I saw. Before me was a continual stream of fire coming from the mouth of the dragon. It burned blue at its source and then turned to yellow and orange. It was before me, and yet it didn't touch me, but instead, split in all directions around me. It was as if an invisible shield of some kind stood between me and the dragon.

I then felt the dragon's grip lessen. I took a deep breath, regained my energy, and drove my sword into the dragon's hand. I then fell to the ground below and was able to evaluate the situation. The ladies were on both flanks of the enemy with their arrows, many aflame, sinking within the dragon's hide. The men were striking the beast down while others from our company were guarding us from the second dragon who remained still. I then witnessed Nathan, his sword shining in the noonday sun, run under the belly of the beast and strike it down dead.

We then turned to the second dragon which snarled at us and seemed to laugh. Its black wings spread and began to send dust swirling around us. Soon it was in the air and making its way to the south. Then it circled back and approached us.

"Dragon's fire!" someone shouted.

Captain Benjamin lifted his voice. "Shield wall!"

We all joined together as one. The men held their shields in every direction, forming a structure like that of a giant tortoise. The women hid under our protection. Soon heat and light encircled us. Then all was still, and the dragon was returning to the mountains.

Fortunately, no one was seriously injured.

"They are growing stronger," Nathan said.

"And yet, in the Great King, we can overcome," pronounced Captain Benjamin. "But," he continued, "I believe you are correct, Nathan. It is obvious that the black dragons have grown stronger. And for this reason, we should go no further in this present campaign. We have killed a black dragon and that is good. I wanted us to go to the mountains, their stronghold, but I think we must be patient. After further training, we will be ready. Everyone get themselves ready to return."

Captain Samuel then approached me. "Are you alright? That was a close one."

"I'm fine," I replied. "But I don't understand. What was that?"

"I believe it was someone's ability," he replied. "An ability they didn't realize they had. I've never seen anything like it."

"Whose ability?" I asked.

Captain Samuel sighed. "It was hers," he said pointing.

Elizabeth stood there, her eyes fixed upon me, with the same look they had when her hands were outstretched. I returned her gaze. Then, remembering myself, I bowed and spoke to her.

"Thank you," I said.

She also bowed slightly. "You are welcome, sir" she said gently.

"Well," Captain Samuel said with a smile, "two new abilities discovered within as many minutes. It seems, Caleb, that you have the gift of discerning the presence of the enemy. That ability will increase as you use it and grow in your knowledge of the Great King. And you, my beloved Elizabeth, have the gift of intervention. You can make a shield around others. I have heard of such abilities but, in all my many years, have never personally witnessed them."

"But, Father," Elizabeth said, "why have I never known this? I have been fighting dragons for years."

"I believe I know the answer to this riddle," he replied. "But that is yet to be seen. Let us now leave this place."

"Will we be able to make it back before the sun sets?" Stephen asked.

"No, but we will have the rest of our company bring us provisions and good company.

He then called two men to his side. "Use your ability now and return to the home base. Inform the others of our current situation and ask them to bring aid. We will meet them tomorrow at the midway camp."

The two men nodded their heads in understanding and were gone as quickly as panthers darting into the forest.

We marched for the rest of that day, weary and bruised. We didn't see any other dragons and by nightfall met up with the rest of our company, mainly wives and children, at the midway camp. We celebrated our victories, enjoyed good food, and warmed ourselves by the fires. I found myself sitting next to Captain Samuel.

"You are attracted to my daughter," he said. "This is obvious. What are your intentions?"

I wasn't sure what exactly to say. I knew my heart, but I was so new to this way of life and was therefore unsure of the correct response.

"I suppose, I would want to marry her," I replied.

"You suppose? There is no room for supposition in such things. You must be sure of your intentions. You are fresh out of the world and the Castle, and therefore, are dangerous in this regard."

"Forgive me," I said. "I don't *suppose*; I *know*. I assure you, sir, that if you knew me better, you would know my heart and mind."

Captain Samuel took a deep breath, and his eyes seemed to travel within the past.

"I know you better than you would ever believe," he said. "I've known your heart even before you were born."

"I don't understand," I said. "How is that possible?"

"Because I knew your grandparents," he replied.

"My grandparents?" I replied. "You mean on my mother's side?"

"Yes," he said. "Your grandfather was my dearest and closest friend."

I couldn't believe what I was hearing. Yet as I worked through those words, everything started to make sense.

"That's why you so quickly accepted me," I said.

"It is," he replied. "I saw the fire in your eyes that I so deeply loved in your grandfather."

"How did you know him?" I asked.

Captain Samuel again paused, his eyes squinting, as if penetrating through the walls of time.

"I was his captain in the Castle. Your grandparents along with your mother attended. I trained your grandparents, took them into the forest, and they died. I barely escaped myself."

I now saw tears in his eyes.

"What happened?" I asked.

"I was a young captain, straight out of one of the Great Castles. I thought I had all the answers. Your grandparents came to my Castle, looking for a new life. They wanted to follow the Great King. They wanted to kill dragons. I fell in love with them. I taught them everything I knew, yet it was all head knowledge without true skill. Then, in my zeal to boast of being a good captain, and in their zeal to kill a dragon, we entered the forest together. The rest I will not tell for it brings me too much grief. Your grandparents, with all their love for the Great King, knew in their last moments on this earth that I had failed them. I had not prepared them for true combat against the enemy.

"The next day, after they were buried, I left the Castle and never returned. I couldn't ever bring myself to look into the eyes of your mother, who was only a small child at the time. She went to live at the orphanage, and I selfishly avoided her, for she was a constant reminder of my failure. But I did keep up enough to know when you were born. Even in your younger years, it was clear to me that you possessed the heart of your grandfather, for I would see you pretend to follow the Great King. I made up my mind to protect you, and one day, to train you. Indeed, on the night of the Great Fire, so many years ago, I came to your house to save you. As I approached, you fell from the window."

"You were the man in the cloak!" I said, remembering back to that fateful evening.

"I was," he said. "But then, after the fires settled, I looked for you and could not find you. I heard that you had gone to the West, and for many months, I searched but came up empty handed."

He then turned to me, eyes full of tears. "I'm sorry for how I failed your family."

It was easy for me to have compassion on this man. I knew the deceit the enemy had brought to the Castles and, I assumed, the Great Castles as well. I understood what it was to step out in faith, thinking you had the correct insight and strategy, only to fail. I knew what it was to let pride convince you that you were one

138

hundred percent in the right with no chance of error, despite many signs attempting to reveal to you the truth.

"There is nothing to forgive," I replied. "You have proven yourself faithful. My grandfather, your old friend, is smiling upon us both."

Captain Samuel wept for a few minutes. The two of us embraced. Even though we were in the midst of the others, they allowed our meeting to be private. We then sat down, ate some more food in silence, and continued our conversation.

Suddenly, I remembered how a Scroll had been left on my porch months prior. I asked Captain Samuel if he had done that. He denied any involvement and quickly changed the subject.

"I will teach you the ways of the Great King regarding how to get to the marriage altar," he said.

"That would be wonderful."

"Listen carefully," he began. "The first thing you must do is dismiss completely the practices of this world, many of which have infiltrated the Castle. The Scroll is all we need. It tells us how to do this according to the will of the Great King. The world, and the Castle, allow their young ones to pretend they are married without the true commitment or covenant. They do mock marriages and then, when they change their minds, mock divorce. This only sets them up for failure, for it desensitizes their resolve for true commitment. And so, after they get married, as soon as challenges arise, they quit, and get divorced, for their many years of mock divorce have prepared them to do so. The way they do things also leads to many forms of immorality. You must follow the Scroll. The rules of the Great King are simple: never be alone with a woman; never touch a woman until she is your bride, with the exception of her hand only in greetings and farewells; and never speak to her as someone more than a sister. In the Scroll, there are only two kinds of relationships between you and a woman: that of a sister and that of a wife. The world and the Castle have created a third kind: pretend marriage; or *linking* as they call it. Linking

139

takes some of the benefits of marriage yet denies much of the responsibility. It is dangerous. This you must utterly reject, for it is from the enemy. Do you understand?"

"Yes, sir. I understand it and I love it."

"Good," he replied. "Concerning Elizabeth...continue to show her respect, and when the opportunity arises, I permit you to speak with her. I am convinced that the two of you are a potential match; therefore, I will allow you to write to her. This, my son, is a special privilege. And should only be done when you are quite certain that you want to pursue marriage. But remember, your writing must be as modest and proper as your behavior and conversation. You may give me any letter you have for her. I will likely read it, and then I will give it to her. Be sure to protect your heart. And most of all, protect hers."

"Yes, sir."

"Do you have any questions?" he asked.

"Only one," I said. "Do you have any paper and ink I could borrow?"

Chapter 23

Fortunately, Captain Samuel always traveled with the instruments for writing, just in case he needed to make notes or send a letter. For a good hour, I sat alone thinking about what to write. In the end, this is what it read:

Dear Elizabeth,

I, as a brother in the family of the Great King, write to you with the highest respect and value for your purity and honor. As for myself, I'm sure it is obvious that I am new to all of this, yet I assure you that I am all in. I am confident and convinced, without any doubt, that I will serve the Great King for the rest of my life. Since I have come under the training of your beloved father, my heart has turned more to family. So now I also dream of one day being the captain of my own family, teaching them to fight dragons, and hopefully becoming a captain in the army of the Great King. I pray that you will be blessed and that the favor of the Great King will be upon you. I have observed you from afar, and I have greatly enjoyed our brief conversation. I pray that I will be allowed to know you more.

Your caring brother,

Caleb

I handed the letter to Captain Samuel just before the company went to sleep. That night, I took the first watch along with Nathan. We visited about all that had happened that day.

"You seem troubled," I said to Nathan. "Aren't you glad to have your children back with you?"

"I am," he replied. "I was just surprised about the black dragons we encountered today. As of late, they've grown larger and stronger."

"Why do think that is?" I asked.

"There's little question as to why," he replied. "It's because the time is short. The end of this age is closing in on us."

"What does that mean?" I asked.

Nathan smiled. "It means that we must fight harder, and we must be more courageous. The Scroll says that the Great King chooses when and where we are born. This means that there are no accidents. We are here, now, for a reason. The Great King is on the move, leading and guiding His armies. Someday, He will actually lead us in person. And on that day, He will find the Great Dragon and slay it. We will, along with Him, destroy the remaining dragons. Then we will rule with Him forever."

"I can't wait for that day," I said.

"It will be here before you know it," he said. "Until that day, we continue to fight, lest we be found on the wrong side in that final battle."

The company was back marching at sunrise and made it to the Oasis by midmorning. For some reason, which I didn't understand, I greatly desired to go to the Castle. Captain Samuel didn't speak against this choice, and looking back, I believe he saw it as a necessary part of my pilgrimage.

I arrived at the Castle just in time for the main ceremony. Their numbers had apparently increased in the past two months, for there was an additional banner in the main hall which read, "1,000 Members Reached!" Providentially, I found myself next to Justin. He greeted me somewhat warmly but with some caution. We sat and listened to Captain David.

"Why do we gather?" he began. "Why do we train? This is an important question, for if we can't answer it according to the Scroll, then we are wasting our time. We gather together and train in the arts of the Great King because that is what He commands. Who here wants to be obedient to the Scroll? I know that all of you do. And this is the good news of today's message. When you come here every King's Day, and when you train in Scroll Class, you are obeying the Great King. This is also why you give a tenth of your income every King's Day; it is in the Scroll..."

As I listened to Captain David's message, I was overwhelmed by how easy it is to be fooled. One of the titles of the Great Dragon was the *Great Deceiver*. I realized, at that moment, just how powerful deceit was. By definition, when someone is deceived they don't know it. Only a few months earlier, I would have sat under the same message, nodding my head in agreement, thinking that I was pleasing my King by my attendance. I would have believed that my supposed training at the Castle was the focus instead of obedience to that training—namely, killing dragons and being a man of honor.

I knew that almost all of the people in the Castle had good intentions but lacked understanding. At that moment, I realized that good intentions were not a reasonable substitute for a lack of understanding. Here were one thousand people, many with noble intentions. They were trying to follow the Great King. They thought that their conduct was from the pages of the Scroll, that the Scroll was dictating their behavior and practices. But instead, they were following a different code of conduct—one decided by men—and they were using the Scroll to justify their practices.

They were wielding the weapons of their choice, NOT because that's what the Scroll said but because that was the common practice of the Castle and of the world. They were dropping off their children at the Younglings Guild, NOT because that is what the Scroll said but because of the world's influence and wicked philosophy. They were satisfied with killing two or three dragons per year, NOT because that was what the Scroll said but because that was the accepted expectation of the Castle. (Actually, it was the captain that killed the dragons, not the Castle.) The standard of this army was no longer the Scroll. Their standard was themselves. I refocused my attention to Captain David's closing remarks.

"So how do we move forward? What do we do? The answer is simple: we bring others into this army. Far be it from us to be selfish with the treasure of the Great King. Far be it from us to be hard-hearted to those who don't experience the blessing of what we do every King's Day. All of you know people who need to join this army. Perhaps it is your neighbor or a family member. Bring them all. Perhaps they've heard that following the Great King is too difficult. We will show them that He accepts everyone, just as they are. Perhaps they have heard that fighting dragons is going to require too much of their time. One day a week isn't too much to give up when you are gaining the Great King's favor. Now, some of you are thinking what I'm thinking, *This Castle is getting crowded.*"

At this, everyone laughed. Captain David continued with a smile.

"Remember the words of the Great King: *On this rock, I will build My Castle.* This is what we are doing. Soon, we will build an army and a Castle that will cause the dragons to flee from the edges of the forest. If each of you brings two people, our numbers will soar to three thousand! We will not ask these people to come and squeeze into this overgrown Castle. We will build a new Castle in its place! The designs have already been made! What say you?!"

Everyone cheered, and the service was concluded with a song. I quickly exited my row and made my way out through the west passage. There were many Scroll teachers sitting around, sipping coffee and laughing. I continued. I then passed the Younglings Guild. The younglings were running around in circles with many young adults around them, like farmhands corralling cattle. I had made up my mind. There was no way to turn around the Castle. It was out of control. The only hope I had was to do things according to the Scroll, to raise my children according to the Scroll, and try to influence others, one family at a time. I then heard someone calling my name. I was shocked when I turned around.

It was Captain David.

Chapter 24

"Caleb!" he called out, walking quickly after me.

I turned to him. He stopped, smiling as he always did, and took a moment to catch his breath.

"I noticed you in the gathering," he said. "It's good to have you back here. I hope you will be joining us again on a regular basis. I was a bit disappointed that you dropped out of the Youngling Guild so abruptly. But I think I understand; you are exploring different options and ideas."

I saw this man in a different light than before. I still considered him a brother and a captain of sorts. But he was no longer an authority figure in my life; in fact, I feared he had misunderstood authority himself in that he was enslaved to the will of men more than the will of the Great King.

"I may come to visit you," I said respectfully. "But this is no longer my home."

"May I ask why?" he replied.

"For the simple reason that this place doesn't focus on fulfilling the will of the Great King as much as I thought it did."

I noticed the shock on his face and I continued. "It may accomplish some good, but the damage is so much more in comparison. The little good does not justify the overwhelming wrongdoing."

"What?" he replied. "How can you even say that? So, are we enemies now?" he asked.

"Absolutely not," I answered. "As the Scroll says, *Your battle isn't against people. It's against dragons.* We are brothers. And I love you dearly. But what you're allowing here is deceitful. It has the look of an army but denies the power thereof."

"What are you even talking about?" he asked. "We have a Castle. We have warriors with swords and bows and shields. This is exactly what the Great King wants!"

My heart was breaking with compassion for this man. He wanted to be a great leader in the army of the Great King but was instead a slave to the people; therefore, he was completely missing the reality of the Scroll. On the surface, he had the appearance of a captain leading the Castle of the Great King, but in reality, he was only leading people into a convenient form of religion. They looked like warriors, but most of them were anything but.

"Yesterday," I said, "I was part of a company that killed a black dragon—a *black* dragon. Most people here don't even know they exist."

"Well, that doesn't surprise me," Captain David said defensively. "Anyone under the training of Samuel can learn to do such things. But you are so few. His many years of devotion have created an army of what, forty people? And not only that, but forty people no one knows about. Not sure if you noticed, but there were over one thousand people here today. And everyone sees us gather. They see our Castle. You don't even have a Castle to speak of."

I felt words come to me from somewhere deep within and did not hold them back but let them flow freely. "Would not the Great King rather see forty people killing dragons than a thousand people pretending they are and nothing more?" I asked. "Would not the Great King like to see husbands and wives fighting side-by-side, in harmony, as the Scroll says? Would not the Great King like to see children wielding the sword and the bow instead of being continually separated from their parents, as burdens to be dealt with instead of future warriors to be poured into? You have been deceived, Captain David. Consult the Scroll. Even the Great King, when He walked this earth, only had a handful of warriors by His side. And they changed the world."

I could see the frustration in David's eyes. He wanted to disagree with me but could find no true basis to do so. "And what would you have me do?" he said at last.

"It is simple," I replied. "First, get your own life in order. Become the warrior you were meant to be. Then, get your home in order. I know your children. They are rebellious and worldly. They do not revere their parents or the Scroll. Lastly, find a handful of families who don't want to play the Castle game but who truly want to train and fight dragons, and devote your life to them."

"You foolish boy," he said. "You think I should just abandon these people? They are all looking to me for guidance."

"Then you must choose," I said plainly. "Either choose to please the Great King or choose to please the people. You cannot do both. You will try and you will fail. You are in slavery to the will of these people. All you care about is whether or not they approve of you and are excited to be in this army. You are like the waves of a storm, brother, always tossed back and forth. You see something in the Scroll, but before you preach it, you ask yourself, *What will the people think?* Instead, you should preach the truth regardless of what they think. Obviously, if they don't receive it, then they aren't followers of the Great King. You should tell them the truth, David, and the few who stick around are the true warriors of the Great King.

"You have a different priority from the Great King," I continued. "He put quality above quantity. He often turned people away because it was obvious that they weren't all in. He doesn't require perfection; He requires only a heart that is truly surrendered. And yet you reverse it; you put quantity above quality. You are following a vision that isn't from the Great King but from men. He wants an army that is pleasing to Him. You want something that is pleasing and impressive to the world. I will pray for you because I believe that deep down you see the truth and I love you. It isn't too late for you to be a true captain of the Great King."

I could see only confusion and frustration in the eyes of my brother. I bowed in respect and turned to leave. He shouted after me. "That's all easy for you to say! You have nothing to lose! I have everything! If I did things the way Captain Samuel does, then they would all leave!"

"That's your choice," I said plainly, as I continued to walk. "You must choose; you must either serve the people or the Great King."

"But they would kill me," he said.

"Then die!" I replied.

I exited the Castle and began to circle around it for the road that led to my home. I was going over the conversation I had just concluded, reviewing what I said. The Scroll tells about how the Great King will sometimes speak through us. I wondered if that had just happened. It was an experience that Nathan had told me about. He said that you will speak words, and then when you are finished, you will go take notes on what you just said. That's how I felt.

I was now surrounded by many others walking home from the Castle. I greatly desired to tell them all to follow me into the forest, down the trail, to the meeting place of Captain Samuel. But I knew that was wrong. It would be no different than Captain David's plan to just bring people to the Castle; people who might not be ready. When did I know someone was ready to bring to the Oasis? This was something I needed to figure out. I trusted the Scroll had the answer.

Quickly I went to my small home, got it in order, ate a quick dinner, and fell asleep from emotional and physical exhaustion. In the middle of the night, something woke me up. It wasn't a noise but a feeling. The sun was barely starting to glow in the east. I went back and forth in my mind whether I should sleep some more or get an early start at my shop in the market. But for some reason, I wasn't able to shake the feeling. It was as if something was very wrong. I suddenly had an overwhelming urge to run to the Oasis. I hesitated. I didn't want to be strange or obnoxious to Captain Samuel or, especially, to Elizabeth. But I couldn't resist.

I grabbed my sword and shield and hurried toward the forest. The morning fog now lay over the countryside. A few people were out and about, getting an early start to their day. I then entered the forest, and in doing so, entered back into the darkness of night. But I knew my way, and I had no fear of dragons, only what I would find at my destination. I finally came into the clearing. I expected to see nothing but the dew of the morning and quiet homes, filled with sleeping people. Instead, I saw about a dozen people gathered mainly around Captain Samuel, who was examining the ground between his home and the forest. Nathan was there. He saw me running toward him.

"Caleb!" he called out. "Hurry!"

"What is it?" I asked as I came near to him.

"Something has happened to Elizabeth," he said. "Captain Samuel was awakened about an hour ago to her screams. He went to her room but she was gone."

"Was nothing found?" I asked.

"Only this," Captain Samuel said, his voice sober and distant, as a man who is awaiting to awake from a nightmare but knows it is impossible. He handed me a letter. "I saw her writing it before I went to bed last night," he added, after which he continued examining the ground. I quickly opened letter. This is what I read:

150

Dear Caleb,

I thank you for your kind letter. And I thank you for your generosity and courtesy for me and my heart. I, like you, wish to serve the Great King for the rest of my life. My greatest desire in my service to the Great King is to be a wife to a noble warrior. I desire to serve him faithfully, to bear many children, and raise them to the glory of the Great King. Of all material possessions, I am most thankful for the Scroll, by which I am able to follow the ways of my King. And now, my brother, what more is there to say except the following: *Down with the Dragon and all his race.*

Your sister,

Lily

It took a full minute of staring at the last line of the letter to understand. Elizabeth was Lily—my childhood friend from so many years earlier. The pretty girl from next door, with whom I pretended that we were the soldiers of the Great King, was now the woman of my dreams. The girl that I loved as a child was now the woman that I loved as an adult. She was back from the dead, as it were, and had captured my heart. At that moment, I didn't consider how this miracle was possible. All I thought about was the fact that she was missing.

"I don't understand," I said. "This letter is kind and sweet. Why would she leave?"

"She didn't leave," Captain Samuel said returning to the house entrance, his eyes filled with sadness and fear. "She was taken."

"Taken?" I enquired. "By whom?"

"By a black dragon," he replied.

Chapter 25

"A black dragon?" I said with a voice of fear, shock, and frustration. "How was a dragon able to enter this grove?"

"It is rare," Captain Samuel replied, "and, unfortunately, so is the return of their victims."

I couldn't believe what was happening. I thought that I was finally finished with heartache and disappointment. After all, hadn't I learned that lesson enough? I had discovered that my childhood soul mate was alive, only to lose her the same moment. Captain Benjamin now arrived, along with others, and was updated on the situation.

"Elizabeth taken?" he asked. "Again?"

"Again?" I said aloud, looking at Captain Samuel. "She's been taken before?"

"Yes," the elder said. "It was the night of the Great Fire when you were young. The next morning, I was unable to find you and had heard rumors that you wandered off to the west. I went that way and picked up the tracks of a young child that had wandered to the edges of the forest. It was evident that a dragon had reached out of the forest and taken the child. I followed its tracks deep within the ranks of the enemy, thinking I was coming to your rescue, only to find a young girl in your place. I was able to rescue her, only barely, and at great peril."

"Why Elizabeth?" asked Nathan. "Why does the enemy want her?"

"That is what we must find out," Captain Benjamin replied.

"What are we going do?" I asked, my heart filled with determination beyond anything I had known.

"There's only one option," Captain Samuel replied. "We must find her and rescue her before it's too late."

"Should I ready the army?" Nathan asked.

"No," replied Captain Samuel. "We are going in with only a few of our most skilled warriors. We will slip through the ranks of the enemy and bring Elizabeth back, hopefully without the knowledge of the enemy."

The aged warrior looked upon those gathered about him.

"I will go," Captain Benjamin said.

"We will go together, my old friend," Captain Samuel said.

"I will go," Nathan said, "if you will have me."

"Are you sure?" asked Captain Samuel. "This mission is perilous. You have a wife and children to think about."

"I understand," Nathan replied. "I feel the Great King leading me to go. I, therefore, have no choice in the matter."

"Very well," replied Captain Samuel. "The three of us leave immediately."

"What about Captain Enoch?" Nathan asked. "He is likely the greatest warrior of us all."

"He has gone on a journey to other villages," Captain Benjamin said. "He is to meet with our brothers and elders abroad and to share with them his vision."

"What vision is that?" Nathan asked.

"That the time will soon come for all of our scattered brethren to unite as one."

I was waiting for Captain Samuel to acknowledge me, but he didn't. I couldn't stay silent.

"I am also coming," I said resolutely.

"I'm not sure that's a good idea," Captain Samuel said. "In fact, I'm quite certain it's not."

"But surely I must!" I replied. "This woman is the love of my life! My true love! That must count for something."

"We will try to bring her home to you," he said.

"I will bring her home," I contested.

"No!" he replied in anger. "The last time you went into the forest, you ended up in the claws of a black dragon, helpless and afraid. The only thing that saved you was the love of Elizabeth!"

"But you just proved my point!" I said, also with passion in my heart, and I felt a flame lit within me. "What you say is true! I was before my certain death. And yet you, Captain Samuel, with all your skill and cunning didn't save me. None of you did! It was the love of Elizabeth that saved me from that dragon. And what if your strength and skill isn't enough to save her, but rather my love—my love for her which burns in me like a fire?"

They all looked at me, speechless.

"The young man is correct," Captain Benjamin said. "Though his skill is lacking, his love is strong. I say that he should join us."

Captain Samuel hesitated, then consented. "Very well. If Captain Benjamin believes this is best, I will follow his leading."

He then turned to Stephen.

"Stephen," he said. "You and your family are left in charge here until we return. Be in continual prayer and stay out of the forest. Blessings and goodbye."

Stephen, along with his son Jedidiah, who stood beside him, bowed in understanding.

"May the power of the Great King go with you," they said.

Within thirty minutes, we were packed, armed, and deep within the forest. Our pace was hurried and we spoke little. That evening we made a quick camp where we would eat, get some sleep, and then continue on at sunrise. As we ate together, I spoke with Captain Samuel.

"I have questions," I said. "How is Lily, I mean Elizabeth, still alive? I saw her corpse, charred and burnt."

"The body you saw was that of a neighbor girl," he explained. "Her parents were going on a trip to the next village, and they left her in the care of Elizabeth's parents. By the time Elizabeth was awoken by the fire, her room was engulfed in flames, and the other girl was nowhere to be found; the neighbor girl likely ran to the room of Elizabeth's parents. Elizabeth escaped her home and running in fear and terror, journeyed too close to the forest's edge. Before she knew it, the dragon came out of the forest and took her prisoner."

"What happened?" I probed further. "After you rescued Elizabeth, when she was a girl, what happened?"

"I took her to her home but her parents were no more. She had no next of kin able to care for her, so I took it upon myself to do so. She told me about you and your friendship, and together we searched for you for many months across the countryside and within surrounding villages. Since we never found you, we came to the conclusion that you died shortly after you had wandered from town.

"You can't imagine our joy, around six months ago, when we heard of your return. And yet, we had to be careful. We didn't know where your heart was. How overjoyed I was that day when you followed me into the forest. Elizabeth wept that evening in my arms tears of joy, for we had both concluded that the Great King had kept your heart true."

I sat and listened with mixed emotions. All in all, my greatest emotion was a longing to see Elizabeth. When I knew her as just *Elizabeth*, I loved her, but now that I knew she was also *Lily*, I was overwhelmed with a deeper love.

"Why didn't you tell me who she was?" I asked. "You could have told me weeks ago."

"That was her decision, as far as when to reveal herself to you," he replied. "And she did it as she saw best. I trust her timing was right and you should too."

We then heard a noise from the pitch-black forest around us. The low glow of the campfire cast a dim shadow upon the surrounding thicket. The four of us stood with our weapons and waited.

"It's a dragon," I said. "I can feel it."

We then saw two objects glowing about twenty yards away from us. They were two eyes, large eyes, peering at us. Soon we could make out the head and face of a red dragon.

"Get ready to engage," Captain Benjamin said softly.

But the dragon didn't advance. It only crouched, still and low to the ground.

"Are any others near?" Nathan asked me. "This one might be a distraction."

"I don't sense any others," I replied. I was about to speak again, but the deep, dark voice of the dragon cut me short.

"I don't come to fight you," it said.

"Then you may be the first wise dragon I've known," Nathan said mockingly.

The dragon continued. "I come to deliver a message."

"We are listening," Captain Samuel said after a pause, his sword and shield still tightly gripped.

"You are wasting your time," the dragon said. "You will not succeed in your mission."

"What mission would that be?" Captain Samuel asked.

The dragon smiled. "The girl."

I felt my blood begin to boil and that at any moment I would jump forward and strike down the beast.

"The girl is out of your reach," the dragon continued. "You will search for her, but you will not find her. You will search for her, but it will be your own doom and destruction."

The dragon then fixed its eyes upon me. "You will never see that girl, ever, ever again."

Chapter 26

I could no longer contain myself. Fear, wrath, and anger were overflowing from the depths of my soul. I leapt forward, my sword swinging down in furry. The dragon was ready, and it turned out, anticipating such a response. It quickly spun around, leaving its head far away from my blow and its tail sweeping around and flanking my attack. I was sent into the surrounding thicket; my sword and shield falling from my hands. I turned to see my three fellow soldiers engage the enemy, and within a moment, the creature was lifeless.

Fortunately, I wasn't injured although my pride had been bruised.

"You fell right into its hands," Captain Samuel said. "It put out the bait and you took it."

"You mustn't allow such anger to enter your heart," Nathan said. "It will only cloud your judgment. The enemy knows this."

"I'm sorry," I said, aware of my shortcoming. "But what about Elizabeth? The dragon said she was beyond finding."

"Dragons are liars," Captain Benjamin said plainly. "They can never be trusted, and their words are usually opposite from reality."

"Deceit and fear," Captain Samuel said. "That is their weapon. I will teach you more tomorrow. Now we must get some sleep if we are to have the energy we need for the journey."

I slept only a little but enough to suffice. An hour before sunrise, we were off again.

"Listen to me," Captain Samuel said as we hurried along. "This teaching is simple yet powerful. Everything in this world—every thought, idea, and action—is either rooted in love or fear. You would like to think that your attack against the dragon last night was rooted in love. The reality, however, is that it wasn't but was rather rooted in fear. You chose to believe the lies of the enemy and therefore allowed fear to enter your heart. This is a tool of the enemy. As long as you act from fear, the enemy has you. Even if your cause is just, and even if you commit your way to the Great King, as long as your heart is filled with fear, you will almost always fail in the end."

"How can I always act in love and not fear?" I asked sincerely.

"You must believe," he replied sincerely. "You must always hang on to the promises of the Great King and the realities presented in the Scroll. Even if everything you see with your eyes appears contrary, it doesn't matter. You must believe. Take this situation for example. What do your eyes tell you?"

I paused for a moment to consider this.

"If I'm honest," I replied, "all I see is despair and hopelessness. I fear that Elizabeth is no more, just as she seemed to be long ago, gone forever, just as my parents and William are gone forever. I fear that I will fail in saving her."

"Yes. That is what you see, Caleb. But what does the Scroll say?"

"I don't know," I replied humbly. With desperation in my voice, I continued, "What does it say?"

Captain Samuel smiled. "It says the Great King is ultimately in control of everything. Nothing happens outside of His ultimate plan. It says that His plans are perfect, and even though they are sometimes difficult for us, His children, they are always good. It says that if He desires us, for example, to find Elizabeth and rescue her, it will happen, guaranteed. It says that if we die in the attempt, it is a noble and good death. In the end, my son, the Scroll says that there is never a reason to be afraid. Never."

"So, I stay away from fear by believing," I repeated.

"Absolutely," my teacher confirmed. "You must believe in the unseen realm. Just as the Scroll says, *Belief is the evidence of that which we don't see.*"

It was beginning to make sense. The ways of the Great King were perfect yet so contrary to the ways of this world. That was what made the army of the Great King such a spectacle to His glory—we believed, even when it seemed like everything was against us.

"And what of love?" I asked. "If belief is the cure for fear, what is the pathway to love?"

"It is the same," Captain Samuel answered. "Just as belief guides you away from fear, so also belief brings you to love. You believe so deeply in the Great King that your love for Him surpasses everything. You love Him and therefore you obey Him. What I am teaching you now, Caleb, will either make you or break you. It is everything. You must train yourself to operate out of love. It is the only way you will succeed."

I knew that Captain Samuel was telling me the truth. I was also certain that even though the concept he had taught me was simple, the application of it would take time. A random question then entered my mind.

"Captain Samuel, what is your ability?"

"The Great King saw fit to make me skilled in training others," he replied.

"And what about Captain Benjamin?" I asked.

"He has the ability of foresight."

"How does that work?" I asked.

"At certain times, when the Great King desires, He shows Captain Benjamin a glimpse of the future or sometimes an understanding of the past."

We were now coming upon the mountains that we had approached only a few days earlier. I was surprised that we had only seen one dragon in the past two days. I sensed that we were moving into a trap. It was as if they were waiting for us to come nearer to their den. I began to see black dragons, in the far reaches of the sky, circling the mountain tops.

"How do we know that she is here?" I asked Captain Samuel.

"Because this is where I found her when she was a child," he replied solemnly. "The enemy rarely changes his strategy. The way they try to destroy us in our youth is usually how they try to destroy us later in life. I must now put into practice the same advice I gave you. My heart is tempted to fear, for we are getting closer."

I couldn't imagine what would be able to tempt Captain Samuel to be afraid. Dragons could be heard now. It seemed that we were coming upon the lairs and dens where many dragons resided. The mountains rose up on all sides of us. We then came upon a narrow lane marked with a stone arch.

"We are here," Captain Samuel said quietly. "And we are fortunate that we haven't had to engage a dragon. Our goal is one of stealth, not might. Down this pathway is a side entrance into the strongholds of the enemy. If this is where they are keeping her—as they did in her youth—then, by the grace of the Great King, we may be able to enter, find her, and get out unscathed."

"Whatever happens," Nathan said, "we must stay together and keep a level head."

"Agreed," said Captain Benjamin. "Better to stand and fight, even if the numbers be against you, then to turn and run. If you run, you will almost always die. We must be brave and, if it comes to it, stand together against all odds."

"Let us pray," Captain Samuel said. "We must ask for the strength and the wisdom of the Great King to go with us."

We bowed our heads to pray and something happened. It was very evident that we were in the presence of greatness. The feeling was so strong that Captain Samuel had a hard time speaking, and for a few seconds, we all just stood in awe of our Great King. Captain Benjamin broke the silence.

"Paper!" he said with urgency, yet still as quiet as possible. "Give me paper, quickly! And a pen!"

Captain Samuel hurriedly supplied the goods needed, after which we witnessed Captain Benjamin kneeling upon the ground, writing frantically. It was evident to me that he didn't know what he was writing, for the script was unreadable. Not only that, but his eyes were closed as he wrote, and his pen strokes were coming from every direction.

"What's happening?" I asked the other two soldiers with sincere concern.

"He is having a vision," Nathan answered. "The Great King is showing him something, something important."

After a few more seconds, it was finished. The captain then opened his eyes, and together we all looked at the paper.

"What is it?" Captain Samuel asked.

"I'm not yet sure," Captain Benjamin replied. "This script is in Scroll ruins."

I knew from Scroll Class that Scroll ruins were the letters of the original Scroll which the Great King penned Himself.

"Can you read it?" I asked.

"Yes," Captain Benjamin answered. "I just need some time. It is about Elizabeth."

Elizabeth! My mind was racing and all my patience fled.

"What about her?" I asked anxiously.

"It speaks of why they want her so badly," he said with a quizzical expression, still trying to make it out. "It seems," he said, "that there is a man and that...."

162

He stopped in the middle of his sentence with a look of shock upon his face. He quickly turned and looked at me, his eyes wide open.

"It's you!" he said.

Chapter 27

"What do you mean?" I asked with both fear and confusion. "What about me?"

"Listen," Captain Benjamin said, looking carefully at the paper. "This is what it reads: The woman is destined to marry her true love. And she will be a helpmeet like no other before her. She will make her husband great. And his destiny will be to lead the people of the Great King into the greatest of all battles."

For a moment, we all just stood there, stunned by such words.

"What are you saying?" I asked.

"It is all making sense now," Captain Samuel answered. "The Great King has chosen you, my son, to be a mighty leader to His people. But you will only reach your true potential by the aid of your wife. The enemy learned of this long ago and has therefore been trying to sabotage the Great King's plan for you by robbing you of your helpmeet."

"But why are they going for her?" I asked in frustration. "Why not come for me?"

"They have," Captain Samuel replied. "In certain times, in certain ways, they have. But this is their way. They often go for the woman, for they know her power. A woman who embraces her role as helpmeet is an unstoppable foe for them."

"But if what you're saying is true," Nathan said, "then we must get Caleb out of here. We must get him back to safety."

"What if it isn't true?" I said, for that was indeed how I felt. I couldn't at all accept the idea of me being a leader in the greatest of all battles.

"It's true," Captain Benjamin testified. "I have never felt such a strong presence of the Great King. I am sure of it. Every word on that paper is true."

"That's why we must get Caleb away from this place," Nathan continued. "He's not ready. We must protect him for the time in which he is ready."

"It's too late for that," Captain Samuel said. "We mustn't divide our forces, and he can't find his way alone. If there's any hope for Elizabeth, we must act now."

"Well, what are we waiting for?" Captain Benjamin asked.

"Come," Captain Samuel said. "It's time to rescue Elizabeth. She is imperative to the survival of our people."

We headed down the shaded, narrow path. The air was still and cool, and at any moment, I feared a terrible dragon coming down upon us. I continued to think about the prophecy that Captain Benjamin had revealed. Could it be true? In a way, it's what I always wanted. But another part of me felt incredibly inadequate, and it caused me to fear. A voice within me said, *Believe My words, and you will triumph.*

We came quickly around a corner and what we saw took my breath away. There was a very large opening which entered the mountain—large enough for a black dragon to enter. Crouching on both sides of the opening were dragons, the likes of which I'd never seen before. They were as massive as red dragons but longer and lower to the ground. Their color was that of a dark purple. They hissed with a violent shaking when they beheld us, and their appearance was so formidable that I nearly fell to the ground. Before we had time to react, one of the

165

creatures wobbled its head and shot out its tongue nearly thirty feet in our direction. The tongue wrapped around Nathan's pack, ripping it from his arms. The creature swallowed the pack as fast as lightning, and I assumed from my brothers' reaction that this was a foe that none of them had ever faced before this moment.

"Shields up!" Captain Samuel ordered.

The second dragon now shot out its tongue, and taking hold of Captain Benjamin, pulled him straight into the creature's mouth. We charged forward in response, hoping we could come to his aid. As I ran toward the dragon opposite me, I waited for his head to shake, for I had noticed that this movement always preceded the lunging of the tongue. The shake happened, and I quickly darted to one side, barely dodging the attack.

Nathan and Captain Samuel were now upon the dragon who had taken Captain Benjamin, but I paid them little heed, for all my attention was on my adversary. I was now within reach of the dragon who swiped at me with its front claws. I blocked the attack with my shield, after which I countered down upon the head of the dragon. My sword hit the beast's eye, causing it to step back. I knew that I didn't want any distance between us, especially with its tongue, so I ran forward, and using a nearby boulder that was about four feet high I sprung myself up into the air and was able to come down with my sword. The creature lay dead, my sword penetrating its head from top to bottom.

I then looked over to find the other dragon being finished off by Nathan. Captain Samuel was holding Captain Benjamin and weeping. I could faintly hear Benjamin's voice.

"Caleb," he was saying. "Caleb."

I quickly ran and knelt beside him.

I could tell that he had little time left in this world, for the dragon had bitten deep within his flesh. Blood was everywhere.

"Here I am," I said.

"Listen to me," he began, as he looked within my eyes and strained for every word. "You must believe. The prophecy is true. You will lead our people. But listen to my final words, for they are also true. You will endure much hardship—more than you have ever known. It will often seem like there's no hope, but do not falter. For just when you think you can go no farther, the Great King will come to you. You must believe, my son. You must believe."

He then looked to Captain Samuel, who was still holding him and weeping.

"Farewell, Samuel. We had good times. I will see you again, my friend, on that final day."

And so, Captain Benjamin, one of the wisest men I had ever known, died. His death was honorable indeed. For some time, we stayed there, unmoved and looking upon our beloved brother and respected captain.

"He was the best man I knew," spoke Captain Samuel. "He rescued me from myself so many years ago and showed me how to truly embrace the Scroll."

"I never knew such a kind man," Nathan said, also weeping. "I will miss him. My sons and daughters will write and sing songs about him—about the honorable life he lived and about the honorable death he died."

After some time, Captain Samuel spoke with his face now unwavering and fearless, "We must linger no longer. Come. We must leave our friend here for a little while. We will return for him. Let's enter the dungeons before us. We will not stop now. It is either victory, or death."

We followed our captain within the underground tunnel. We soon lit torches. Around every corner I feared the worst. I whispered to Captain Samuel as we trekked through the foul and lifeless passageways.

"What were those dragons?" I asked quietly.

"I'm not sure," he replied. "Likely a special breeding of the enemy. They were fierce, and I hope we don't run into any more like them."

We soon entered an enormous cavern. It was so large that our torches failed to illuminate it entirely. I could make out another tunnel, as large as ours, connected to the opposite end of the cavern. I then heard a voice—her voice—and in the dark of that hellish den, it was as a rainbow bringing joy to my heart.

"Who's there?" she asked gently, with fear in her voice.

"We are here," I answered softly, not wanting to draw attention to any dragons who might be near.

Her voice was coming from high above, and holding our torches over our heads, we could barely make out a cage suspended from the center ceiling of the cavern.

"I think I see a rope of some kind," Nathan said. "I think it is holding her to the ceiling of the cave over a pulley and is tied off on the far side of the cavern."

"We should be able to lower her down," Captain Samuel said.

My heart began to lift, for it seemed that we were only a moment away from releasing Elizabeth and escaping back to our homes.

But then I sensed something, something big and more dangerous than I had before. A sound now emerged. And we knew it all too well. It began with breathing and footsteps. Because of the lack of light, we could only make out bits and pieces of what we saw, but it was evident that a dragon was entering through the tunnel on the opposite end of the cavern. What was confusing to me was the size. I could roughly make out the dimensions of the dragon, and they were nearly double of any dragon I'd seen before. I wondered if Nathan and Captain Samuel were just as surprised. My curiosity was soon settled.

"That's the largest dragon I've ever seen," Captain Samuel said plainly. "We must stay together, and we must be strong."

A deep voice then echoed throughout the cavern. It was the dragon.

"What fools you are to come here," it said.

"Is that *the* Dragon?" I asked fearfully.

"No," replied Captain Samuel. "The Great Dragon will not show himself until the last battle."

We took a step toward the dragon, who was now standing still, only a small distance from Elizabeth's cage, which was suspended about the same height as the beast's head.

"What fools," it said again. "I know of your prophecy, Caleb."

The mention of my name, coming from the dragon's mouth, made me tremble slightly.

"I've been following you since you were young. This is not our first meeting. I lured you into the forest one day, disguising myself as a beautiful woman. And oh, how you loved me. Ha! All of this prophecy was supposed to end that day, if not for those foolish hunters."

As the dragon spoke, his words took me back to that day; Elizabeth and I being tricked by a dragon, being lured to our doom.

"Didn't you all think it strange that forces of dragons didn't try to stop you from coming here? Trust me, they wanted to. But I told them to stay away, for I wanted you all to myself. And now, Caleb, I'm going to kill you. Your true love, this girl, will watch you come to nothing, and the prophecy will be undone. The other men, who were foolish enough to come with you, will be imprisoned here for the rest of their days. They will rot in this darkness."

Many things happened all at once. I heard a sound from above us like a latching of metal. After I briefly glanced up and back around, I saw Nathan extend his palm out to me in a violent motion. Regardless of him being six feet away, I was sent flying away from him and Captain Samuel. A large cage then fell upon them both, while I landed upon the hard, stone floor, beaten and out of breath. They were imprisoned, and I was alone to face the dragon. I then heard the beast laughing quietly to himself as he strode in my direction.

Chapter 28

Fear. That is all that I felt in that moment. I was without the aid of my friends and was against the most formidable opponent any of us had ever faced. I felt alone, inadequate, and empty.

The dragon then took in a deep breath.

"Dragon fire!" Nathan shouted. "Make ready!"

We held up our shields but no fire came. Instead, a strong and ice-cold wind came from the dragon's mouth. Our torches were suddenly extinguished and we couldn't even see our hand in front of our eyes.

"I can't see!" I shouted aloud.

"Exactly," the dragon replied. "You've never been able to see, Caleb. You've been blind your entire life. And because you've been so blind, look at all who have suffered. You couldn't save your parents. Neither could you save William. And now, you forsake your true love and your dearest friends. Everything you ever believed was a lie. The Great King is nothing. Where is He? You will look, but you won't find Him, for He isn't even real. But I am real. And I am your death."

There I was, on my own against the fiercest dragon any in my army had encountered. All was pitch black. The words the dragon was speaking were the same words I'd told myself many times. They were my story; I was a failure and I was alone. But then I recalled the words of Captain Benjamin. *You must believe,* were his final words to me. I remembered that the dragons only speak lies. I remembered that the Great King was in control and that His ways were perfect. And as the dragon continued to speak, from somewhere deep within me a new story immerged.

You can see, My son. Even in the darkest shadows, you can see. I have made you alive, and I have given you My sight. You were a faithful son to your parents. You were a faithful friend to William. And you are a faithful brother and hero to Elizabeth. I am with you, Caleb. I will fight for you. Do not be afraid. Be strong, for He that is in you is greater than any dragon.

I stood in the darkness, unafraid and unmoved by the empty threats of my foe. I was free. I held up my sword and a light shone forth. It was bright, and it caused the giant dragon across from me to cover his eyes with his claws and groan aloud.

"You are wrong," I said. "The Great King is alive. He lives in me. And you, therefore, are fighting an enemy beyond you. Today we will all leave here, free and together. Your carcass is the only thing that will rot in this darkness."

The dragon lunged at me in anger. I dodged its attack and was able to strike its claw, causing it to cry out in pain. I quickly began sprinting around the perimeter of the cavern. I heard the dragon breathe deeply. This time it was fire. I held my shield as I ran. I could feel much of the flame passing around my lower legs, but it didn't slow me down. I came upon the rope which was connected to the pulley high above. I cried out to Elizabeth. "Hold on!" And grabbing the rope with one hand, I severed it with my sword. I was quickly jerked high into the air and in the direction of the dragon. I was now soaring through the air, at the same level of the dragon's face. It opened its mouth to either devour me or breathe fire. I saw the flames kindled deep within its throat.

I cried out, and the light from my sword grew brighter than any dragon could dare look at. I swung down upon the beast, my blade sinking within its left eye. It cried out in immense pain, the sound nearly shaking the cavern walls. Somehow—I think only by the power of the Great King—I was able to land upon the ground without breaking my legs.

I stood up, the light still shining from my sword. The dragon was backing away from me, holding on to its face, blood pouring from the wound I had inflicted.

"Let that be a lesson to you!" I shouted. "The Great King is sovereign."

"You will never escape this place," the dragon said in anger. "I swear it. I have waited years for this moment! I will not lose it now!"

"Oh, yes, you will," I testified. "For you are foolish enough to come against servants of the Great King."

Anguishing in pain, the dragon continued its retreat. "You will see me again, Caleb!" he shouted. "The prophecy will not come true! This isn't over!"

The dragon then disappeared into the opposite tunnel. I turned and looked around me. Elizabeth's cage was broken open from the fall, and though she was bruised, her body was healthy and unbroken. I wanted so badly to sweep her off the ground and embrace her and hold her tightly, but something within me was awake and aware. I knew how to treat a daughter of the Great King. I offered her my hand, which she graciously accepted, and I helped her to her feet.

"Ms. Elizabeth," I said gently, "let's get you back home."

"Thank you, sir," she replied with a smile. "I am most grateful."

We ran together to the cage which held Nathan and Captain Samuel. It was extremely heavy and we couldn't lift it. After a time of trying, Captain Samuel bid us to leave.

"Get out of here while you can," he said. "You two are all that matter. We aren't worth dying for. The dragon will surely come back with reinforcements."

"He's right," Nathan said, his eyes filled with pain at the knowledge that he wouldn't return to his family. "Caleb," he said. "You must be a father figure to my children, until the Great King supplies them with another father."

"And you must lead our people," Captain Samuel said, "you and Captain Enoch, together. You have proven yourself today. The prophecy was true. Leave now. Hurry, before it's too late!"

I looked over at Elizabeth whose eyes were full of tears and then returned my gaze to my brothers.

"You taught me better than that," I said. "I will not abandon you."

"But you must!" Captain Samuel said. "Obey me!"

I stood back from the cage and gripped my sword.

"On the first night of my training, you told me that courage and faith in the Great King was the sharpness of my blade. Let's see how sharp this blade is."

I then swung down upon the cage with all my might. Sparks flew and the bars were cut. I swung two more times. The same thing happened, leaving a man-sized hole in the side of the cage.

"Let's get out of here," I said.

We retraced our steps and found Captain Benjamin where we left him. Nathan, the largest and strongest of us all, took his captain upon his back and we continued on. We moved quickly but quietly. Our hope was to get out of the sight of the mountains before the alarm was raised. We were out from the mountains' shadows when we heard a deafening dragon cry.

"The alarm!" Captain Samuel shouted. "Hurry!"

As we ran along, as best we could, I could see dragons flying in our direction and could hear the rumble of dragons upon the ground pursuing us. Within a few moments, our retreat was nearly cut off.

"We will have to fight them!" I said. "Stand together!"

Nathan gently set Captain Benjamin to the ground and the four of us stood back-to-back in a circle. Soon there were five red dragons and six black dragons surrounding us. I doubted that even Captain Samuel had ever been engaged by such a number of foes. We raised our weapons. The dragons all inhaled at the same time and simultaneously breathed their fire upon us.

Chapter 29

The light from the dragon fire was brighter than the sun, and we all expected to be left to nothing. But once again, Elizabeth withheld the flame of the enemy. I turned and saw her, palms lifted upwards, bringing an invisible shield around us all. The flame ended and she dropped to the ground exhausted. Our enemies realized that their fire wouldn't be able to win, so they began to creep closer. I knew that there was little hope of us being able to withstand so many, but my heart was resolved and my fear was gone.

"Fight well, brethren," I said to my fellow soldiers. "It's been an honor to fight beside you."

Nathan laughed, his wonderful faith and heart shining through his face. "And it will be an honor to die with you," he said. "I've always wanted a good death. This will definitely be a good one."

The dragons all crouched low, getting ready to pounce upon us together, when suddenly a wave of arrows came into the fray. The dragons spun around, in both pain and surprise, to behold about thirty warriors of the Great King advancing upon them.

"It's Stephen!" I said with joy.

"Fight!" Captain Samuel shouted, and together we advanced upon the nearest dragon.

Another wave of arrows, many aflame, struck many beasts, and men were swinging their swords down upon them.

Nathan and I struck down a red dragon, though in doing so I took a slash to my right side. I then turned to see a sister bring Elizabeth her bow and arrows. My true love immediately began emptying her quiver. She was like a whirlwind of fury, and many dragons were blinded and lame from her wrath.

Stephen raised high his sword, and bringing it down with a shout, he struck the ground. There was a rumbling like an earthquake all around us, but it somehow only affected the dragons. Many of the beasts lost their balance and fell to the ground, giving those nearby the advantage to finish them off. Jedidiah, Stephen's brave son, was also fighting furiously. He had somehow obtained two swords, and was cutting down any dragon that stood before him. Soon a dragon call was given, and all beasts retreated. The soldiers of the Great King let out a shout.

I wanted to celebrate, but the wound on my side was deep. Elizabeth came to my aid.

"You are bleeding severely," she said with concern. She then turned and called out, "Angela!"

A young woman came to us and Elizabeth showed her the wound. The woman touched my side, and I watched with amazement as the wound began to close.

"You should be fine," Angela said.

"Thank you," I said to her, still amazed at her ability. She bowed with a smile and went back with the others.

"You came for me," Elizabeth said. "I knew you would."

I was going to reply but was cut short by Captain Samuel, who embraced me with much rejoicing.

"You did it, my son!" he said. "You were right. Without you, we wouldn't have made it."

He then turned his attention to Stephen.

"Stephen!" he shouted with joy. "What are you all doing here?"

Stephen laughed. "Saving your lives."

"But why?" Captain Samuel asked. "What gave you the idea to come out here and risk so much?"

"We were following orders," Stephen replied.

"Whose orders?" Captain Samuel asked. "Not mine, for I told you to stay out of the forest."

"The orders of the Great King," Stephen replied. "He spoke to us through prayer and bid us come to your aid."

Captain Samuel looked about him once more, beholding all the dragons in retreat. He then looked back at Stephen and smiled.

"Come here, my brother," he said, gesturing an invitation to kneel, "for this is long overdue."

Stephen approached his captain and knelt before him with head bowed.

Captain Samuel knighted him saying, "You have been leading as a captain would for a long time. Now rise and be recognized. I present to you all, Captain Stephen!"

Everyone cheered. The celebration had a bitter end, however, with the discovery of Captain Benjamin's death. But all present knew that it was a good death, and we carried him upon our shoulders as we made our way back home. I walked along in a daze, as if in a dream. Dragons had been hunting both Elizabeth and myself since our childhood. We had been chosen by the Great King to be together and to lead our people in the final battle. I had single-handedly defeated a black dragon of immense proportion and had overcome fear and disbelief.

A smile came to my face, for I realized that I was indeed living my life-long dream. I was a warrior. I was going to marry Elizabeth, and I was going to be a captain of the Great King. I then saw, more than before, the wisdom of Captain Samuel's words. He had told me that the ways of the Great King don't always make sense but that they are always good. And I then realized that all of my life was a series of events that not only brought me to this place, but, more importantly, all of the events of my life had made me the man that I was. They were lessons I needed to learn, truths I needed to understand, and the Great King had orchestrated everything just perfectly to show them to me.

That evening as we made camp, I asked Captain Samuel for permission to speak with Elizabeth. He consented and arranged for us to speak next to the main campfire, still close to others, but where our conversation would be able to be uninterrupted. Our two forms stood only a slight distance from each other.

"Hello," I said.

"Hello," she replied, her eyes and smile lighting my soul.

I invited her to sit and we sat across from each other, the first time we had been alone together for ten years.

"I have so much to say to you," I began. "So many feelings and thoughts. I thought you were dead all these years, and so a part of me has also been dead. But when I found out you were alive, that same part of me was resurrected."

She smiled. "It was the same for me," she said, her gentle force carrying me about with every emphasis of each syllable. "I likewise thought you to be dead. And oh, the joy when I discovered you were alive. And even more joy when I saw you first enter our camp that day."

"You were there?" I asked. "I didn't remember seeing you that first day."

"When I first saw you enter our meeting place," she explained, "I ran into my home and wept. Then that evening, as Nathan and my father gave you your first lesson with the sword, I hid myself and watched, my face beaming with joy and pride at you."

I wanted so badly to tell her I loved her, and the words almost leapt from my lips, but I restrained myself. "There are words I want to say," I said. "But they must wait."

"You can take your time," she said. "I will be waiting."

"You have become a skilled warrior," I said. "Captain Samuel has trained you well."

"My heart was first motivated out of vengeance for my parents," she explained, "and also vengeance for how the dragon's fire separated us."

"You believe a dragon started that fire?" I asked.

"I know it," she said, her face hardening a bit. "I could hear the dragon sniffing at my window."

"But what allows them to leave the forest?" I asked.

"Ultimately," she said, "it's the doing of the Great King."

"The Great King?" I repeated curiously.

"Oh, yes," she said, her smile returning. "And that is how my vengeance was soothed, for I discovered that all things work together according to His plan, even the dragons. They think they are doing their own thing, but they are ultimately His pawns in bringing about something greater than any of us could imagine."

I nodded with appreciation and admiration. The Great King had turned this girl into a woman of wisdom, modesty, and beauty.

"Why did you change your name?" I asked.

"For two reasons. First, to throw the dragons off of my scent. Second, it was a new start for me. I had no real family left, and so Samuel took me in as his own. He named me Elizabeth. It means *Consecrated of the Great King*."

"I like it," I said. "Though Lily was also a beautiful name."

"Thank you," she said. "It's been so long since I've heard that name. It is sweet, but it is no longer me. Please call me Elizabeth."

"Absolutely," I replied. "I have another question. The Scroll I found on my porch, did you do that?"

She smiled. "That was one of the most precious and also the most dreadful days of my life," she said. "I left the words of the Great King upon your doorstep, knowing not whether they would awaken your soul or not."

"My true journey to the light began when I read the words of that Scroll," I said with gratitude.

Captain Samuel now approached us. "Forgive me," he said. "But we must get some sleep. It's been a long day, and we need our rest for tomorrow's journey.

I said goodnight to Elizabeth and soon fell fast asleep.

The next day, we traveled on and reached the meeting place by mid-afternoon. That evening, under the open stars, we buried our beloved Captain Benjamin. Many words were shared. Tears were shed. Laughter was heard. The most touching words were that of Captain Samuel. "When I was young and realized my need to actually train for victory, I met Benjamin. He was young, like me. He hungered and thirsted for righteousness, like me. And like me, he was alone and in need of fellowship. The Great King brought our paths together, and for nearly forty years, we have trained and fought as one. Now, he goes to the eternal barracks of the Great King, in whose mighty company he will be welcomed and blessed. Let us all remember the example he gave us, and let us always honor his memory because he gave his life for his people."

I did not see Elizabeth again that evening, for she was so exhausted that she quickly put herself to bed. I was, myself, too tired to make the trek to the village and my own bed, so I simply lay down by the gathering fire and quickly fell asleep.

I woke early with the sun and suddenly had it in my mind to go to the Castle, for it was King's Day. This idea was surprising, for I had such peace and purpose with my brothers in the Oasis. I questioned my motives and realized that my love for my brothers and sisters at the Castle drew me to them. I thought of my grandfather and how he longed to fight dragons but was never adequately prepared. Many of the people in the Castle were just there to check the box of the Castle's low expectations. But many others truly wanted to know the Great King and serve Him. I wanted to share with them the victory I had discovered. I wanted to tell them how the Scroll worked, if only they would put it into practice. I thought of Captain David, learning all I had learned and passing it on to his people. What an impact they would make for the Great King!

I quickly made my way home, washed up and changed clothes. I then began to head to the Castle, refreshed and encouraged. My true love was safe and I had her heart. The morning air was crisp and clear. People were beginning to emerge and go about their day. I pictured the dragons, frustrated and frightened, crouched down in their dens. It put a smile on my face. I was with the Great King. He loved me and was fighting for me.

I was now approaching the Castle. As I looked up, I saw something at the entrance of the Castle that made me stop and unsheathe my sword. I thought I was dreaming. At the entrance, with people crowded around, was Captain David. Next to him was a dragon.

Chapter 30

I approached cautiously, sword drawn and shield ready. As I neared them, I could see that the dragon wasn't being aggressive but was chained to a stake in the ground. People surrounded the red dragon, gazing and pointing as Captain David continued to speak. I couldn't make out his words. Captain David then went within the Castle, and Eric took over as watchman of the dragon. There were about one hundred people or so around the beast, which was middle-sized, very still, and timid.

"This is the way of the future," Eric was saying, his face beaming with pride. "But Captain David will explain everything today during the meeting."

Eric's eyes met mine as I entered. Behind them was a look of contempt and division. I knew that I was known amongst the leadership of the Castle as being a rebel. I had to remind myself that even though they made me an enemy, I only had one enemy: dragons. I had to remember that I fought for Eric and Captain David and others; I fought so that they might be free.

I went in and quickly sat down. Justin came and sat beside me. Justin was always a comfort to me when I went to the Castle. Even though I knew he was disappointed in me and that he disagreed with my changing perspectives, he still seemed to be friendly and accepting. The Great Hall was filled to the brim, and everyone seemed to be talking about the dragon. Then the service began. After we sang a song and stated our allegiance, Captain David came onto the stage.

"Good morning. I know that many of you were quite amazed, and perhaps even a bit frightened and confused, by what you saw this morning as you entered. Take another look."

The dragon was then led onto the stage by a few of David's men. The beast was leashed by a giant chain and seemed to be willing to obey. The congregation murmured and gasped.

Captain David continued. "For many centuries we have been fighting these dragons, and rightly so, for that is what the Great King has commanded us to do. But I believe that we have evolved in our training and warfare to a point that has never before been experienced. We may still kill dragons from time to time. But why kill something that can be tamed?"

He then looked at the dragon and commanded it to come. The dragon rose to its feet and slowly obeyed. The congregation watched in awe and the murmuring continued. Captain David then commanded the dragon to lie down at his feet, and the dragon obeyed. He then began to pet the dragon, and I was reminded of Edgar and Joseph with the baby dragon in the forest.

"Look!" he said. "This dragon is no longer a threat. Is it still the enemy? Perhaps. But is it still dangerous? Not at all. And this is what many of you have been longing for. Killing a dragon is difficult enough for me having had the training I have, which isn't available for you. So how unfitting is it for me to expect you to kill dragons? And this expectation has discouraged many of you. But look! Wouldn't you want to be able to tame a dragon? To make it obey you as its master? After all, if the dragons don't hurt anyone, what's the problem with having them around? Some of you might be thinking that you can't tame a dragon. Watch this."

Captain David then invited a young lady up to the stage. I recognized her instantly. It was Mary, the widow, who we had helped those many months before. Another dragon was brought out, a bit smaller than the first. Mary commanded the leashed dragon to do certain things and it obeyed her.

After her fourth command, she turned to the congregation and spoke. "For years, I felt so guilty and ashamed that I couldn't destroy a dragon. I was plagued by the reality that the Scroll told me to do something that I wasn't doing. But now, through the simple training of the Castle, I am free from guilt. I can tame a dragon and it will obey me. I still carry my sword and shield, but this leash is my new weapon. And I would encourage you, my brothers and sisters, to join us in this cause. If you join with us, we will go from killing a few dragons a year to taming hundreds if not thousands. What say you? Will you join us?"

The congregation burst out cheering. Captain David and Mary raised their hands in celebration and then commanded their dragons to do the same. The audience erupted with jubilation all the more. I couldn't believe what I was seeing. As I looked around, I noticed Edgar and Caroline, exceedingly happy. I looked behind me and everyone was jumping up and down with enthusiasm. I saw Simon, who was clapping his hands in amazement. I felt all alone. I hadn't thought that things could get worse regarding the Castle, but they just did. I looked at Justin who was still beside me, expecting him to also be rejoicing, but he wasn't. He stood there, still and thoughtful, with a look of confusion and dismay. He then looked at me.

"I don't understand," he said. "I don't think this is right."

"It isn't right," I said to him earnestly. "It's very wrong. It goes completely against the Scroll."

"But," he said, looking around him, "surely Captain David knows what he's doing. He's been to a Great Castle. This must be something good."

I could see his mind wrestling back and forth. I wouldn't relent until I helped him win.

"Listen to yourself," I said. "Quit talking about Captain David or the Great Castles. Think about the Scroll. It's the standard, remember? The Scroll is perfect; we are not. Does the Scroll speak of taming dragons? Does the Scroll speak of dragons being in the Castles of the Great King?"

"No," he said fearfully. "It doesn't. But what if Captain David is right? I've never killed a dragon. I don't honestly think I ever will. But I could tame one, I suppose."

"No!" I said passionately. "The Scroll is true. Why would the Great King ask you to do something that was impossible? He asked you to kill dragons, and dragons you will surely kill. You only lack the proper training. I saw many dragons slain this week, some of them by my own hand. And yet it has nothing to do with me. It is the Great King, living in me through the truths of the Scroll. Trust me, brother. Please! Don't give in to this nonsense."

The congregation was now calming down, and Captain David continued.

"We have a signup parchment in the entryway. All of those who want to experience this victory over the enemy can register. Tomorrow we will begin training, and in only a few weeks, you will be taming dragons. I know you are all eager to get started so we will dismiss. I will see you all soon, and remember, our goal is to keep growing and to build a larger Castle. Tell your friends and neighbors about this. Tell them that if they come to the Castle, they will see dragons tamed. They will love it! Farewell."

The army was dismissed, and Justin and I continued our discussion.

"I need to be alone," he said. He looked as if he was ill.

"I will pray for you," I said. "I will be praying that you will let the Scroll, and not man, be your standard."

Justin walked away and I looked about me. People were everywhere talking about what they had seen. Others were up at the stage looking at the dragons and

185

talking with Mary and Captain David. Others were lining up for the training. I then felt a hand on my shoulder. It was Eric.

"I sure do hope you will sign up for this amazing training," he said with a smile that seemed anything other than sincere.

I hesitated. I didn't know whether to nod my head and escape or to be truthful with him. I decided then that I was done tip-toeing around the truth. I would be honest, with love and respect, just as the Scroll commanded.

"I will most certainly not sign up for such training," I said, "for it goes completely against the Scroll."

"Well," he said with a disapproving glance, "I don't see how you could have the audacity to say such a thing. I think it is perfectly aligned with the Scroll."

"The Scroll says nothing about taming dragons," I said.

"That is exactly your problem," Eric replied. "You are just like the other rebels you associate with. You are all so narrow minded. Does the Scroll say that it is wrong to tame dragons? Not at all. You think that just because something is absent in the Scroll that it is wrong?"

"The issue isn't that it's absent," I said. "The issue is that it goes completely against the commands of the Great King. He commanded death to the dragons, with no exception of any kind. He said that He hates dragons. These dragons entered the world through our bad decisions. He doesn't want us to find peace with them but to kill them. What you're doing is dangerous. And it will only get worse."

"I don't even know why you come around here," Eric said.

"You don't need to," I replied. "It's a Castle. I'm a warrior. That's reason enough. What I don't understand is how you call yourself a warrior of the Great King when you've never even engaged a dragon. You are tricking yourself, Eric. It's exactly what the dragons want. You think you are taming them. You are playing right into their hands. Their plan is to reel you in, gain your confidence, and then destroy you."

I turned around and headed for the door. I noticed Simon and his son, Edgar, along with Caroline standing in a circle of people and talking joyfully. I continued past. Justin approached me.

"There are others who are unhappy with this," he said.

"Good," I replied. "It is likely because they have the Spirit of the Great King inside of them. Tell them to meet tomorrow morning at my home."

"I will," Justin replied. "A part of me thinks you might be right in all of this. But it's hard. I just can't conclude that the Castle is wrong."

"I understand your struggle," I replied. "Trust me. But this is the hard truth. If someone or something is speaking in opposition to the Scroll then they are in the wrong. It doesn't matter who or what they are. No one is immune to heresy or misunderstanding."

"But," he said, still wrestling in his thoughts, "look around. They all have such good intentions."

"Good intentions cannot replace truth," I said, the words coming from somewhere deep within me. "Evil has always hidden behind the guise of *good intentions*, even within the first temptation in the garden. Go and think on these things. And stay close to the Scroll. I will see you and the others tomorrow morning at my home. Be there."

I was only a few steps away from leaving Justin when Captain David approached me.

"I know you don't approve," he said, seemingly wanting to get in the first word.

"David," I said with pity in my voice. I was so unsure of this man. Was he deceived or was he openly against the Great King in his heart? *It had to be the former*, I thought to myself. "How do you justify this?" I asked. "Such blatant disobedience to the Scroll?"

"Disobedience?" he said. "Didn't you see the look on Mary's face? That poor woman has suffered for years under the weight of the dragons, only now to overcome them."

"But she hasn't overcome them, David," I said with frustration in my voice. "It is a lie. They will overtake her in the end. If you don't do things according to the Scroll, in the end they will not work."

He sighed and looked away from me in thought. Could he be questioning his actions? I saw a glimmer of hope.

"You are a good leader," I said. "The people love you and trust you. But don't lead them astray. Stay true to the Scroll and the Great King. You can't fear the people, David. You must trust in the Scroll, no matter what the result. It isn't about what people think or about how they feel. It's all about the will of the Great King, given to us in the Scroll. I believe in you, David. I believe that you can lead these people to true freedom and victory, not the counterfeit freedom you preached to them today."

He looked back at me and began to speak but stopped. He seemed to be wrestling with his thoughts. "Caleb," he began, his voice desperate and in need of help. A young woman then came and interrupted him.

"Captain David," she said, with gratitude in her voice. "You have no idea how I have longed for this day. Always I was ashamed by my lack of ability to fight dragons. My guilt was overwhelming that I wasn't being obedient to the Scroll. But now that shame and guilt is gone. I signed up for the class and can't wait to tame a dragon. Thank you so much, Captain. You are the best thing that ever happened to this Castle."

The woman then walked away. Captain David looked at me, and the look of desperation was gone. The look of determination had returned.

"You don't understand," he said. "You're still young. And I'm tired of trying to make you understand." Then he walked away.

I left the Castle and hurried back to the Oasis, for I greatly desired to speak with Captain Samuel. Many were assembled in there, though all resting, for they were all still weary from the previous day's battle. I told Captain Samuel and those near to him all that happened. He was quiet for a moment, then spoke.

"Taming dragons," he said. "This is a dangerous idea, for it is only one step away from something far worse. I wish I had Benjamin's wisdom and foresight. But the Great King knows best."

"What is it only one step away from?" I asked.

"I dare not say," he replied. "Let us hope that it never comes to pass, the thoughts that are now in my mind. But it is like dominoes. When you line them up, and push the first one, you start a chain reaction. It shouldn't surprise us that they are taming dragons. When you pervert the words of the Scroll, you end up with further degrees of heresy."

"What should we do?" Nathan asked.

"We should wait," Captain Samuel replied. "This is actually, in a way, good news. For as the Castle continues in the downward spiral, the true followers of the Great King who are within the Castle will wake up. I know that there are true followers at the Castle. Let us hope this opens their eyes."

"It is," I said with excitement. "Justin, my friend I've told you about, is displeased about this and is waking up to the truth. He says that many others are as well. I told them to meet me at my house in the morning."

"Well done," Captain Samuel said. "I will be there with you to greet them. We will preach to them the true message of the Great King. And all who are willing will come here with us, and we will welcome them and train them. This might be a bountiful harvest for the army of the Great King. We must be ready." He turned and called out, "Captain Stephen."

"Yes, sir," Captain Stephen replied.

"We must ready ourselves for the possible addition of many to our numbers," he said. "Though I would be shocked if it was more than a few, we must still prepare. I sense that the Great King is purging the Castle. We must be ready to receive any of our true brethren."

"I will begin at once," Captain Stephen replied and immediately began the preparation. I was so impressed by this man, a husband and father, a leader to the people. He had never been to a Great Castle and somehow had a style of leadership superior to those who had received formal education.

"How is it," I asked Captain Samuel, "that we have captains that have never been to the Great Castles?"

"You know the answer to that," he replied with a smile.

"Yes," I replied. "Because it isn't in the Scroll. But how are men like Stephen made without the Great Castles?"

"The same way you are being made," he replied. "By the challenges and lessons of life. As far as the Scroll is concerned, life itself is the Great Castle where leaders are made. The idea of sending our young men off to some place where they sit behind a table, listen to lectures, and somehow return a leader is a very worldly idea. Leadership is learned through trial and conflict and is best taught in the context of close mentor relationships, not distant commanders and scholars. Consider the Great King Himself. He trained up His followers within the context and trials of daily life.

"Besides, the Great Castles don't teach the Scroll as much as they teach the latest ideas of men. It is a dangerous place. But here within the community of the people of the Great King and within the context of family and mentorship is where we make tomorrow's leaders. Truth be told, if one raises his sons in the ways of the Great King, then those men will definitely be captains of valor and truth."

We discussed many other things as well, though my mind quickly turned to Elizabeth who was there within the meeting circle. The council soon concluded, and Elizabeth and I walked around the circle of the meeting place, as was acceptable.

"These are strange times," she said. "It is hard to believe that dragons are within the Castles and yet, in another way, not that hard to believe."

"One thing is certain," I said. "I'm confident that things are about to change. I don't know how exactly. But dragons being led out of the forest and entering the Castles must be a sign that something big is coming."

"And you are going to be an important part of it all," she said.

"I suppose that's true," I said, "according to the words of Captain Benjamin."

"You will need sons," she said. "All good captains, if it is the will of the Great King, have sons beside them."

"That's true," I said. And at that moment, as I said those words, I knew that I was ready to begin my journey with Elizabeth as my wife. Not only was I ready, but I didn't want to put it off for even one more moment. I turned to her and looked within her eyes, "I asked your father for your hand only two days ago, and he said yes. So now I ask you. Will you marry me? Will you stand by my side?"

"With all of my heart," she replied, her face radiating with beauty. "I will stand with you. I will fight with you. I will follow you in complete submission, with reverent respect. I will give you sons and daughters. I will do all I can to serve you. I only have one request."

"Anything," I replied.

"Marry me quickly," she said.

I smiled. "The new moon is less than a fortnight away. On that day at sunset, we will be husband and wife."

Chapter 31

The brethren rejoiced at the news of our union, and we feasted into the evening. Elizabeth and I refrained from any physical affection, as was appropriate, and spent most of our time celebrating, she with the women and I with the men.

I soon found myself around a campfire with all of my dearest friends. Captain Samuel, Nathan, and Stephen were those present along with others.

"Being a husband is a man's greatest calling," Captain Samuel said as we all listened under the moonlit sky. "A husband is called to love his wife and protect her as the Great King would. A husband must lead his wife gently and nobly. He must show her deference. He must put her needs before his own and be willing to die for her if it is necessary."

He then looked at me and smiled.

"The Great King has given you a wise woman, Caleb. Yield to her wisdom. Do not let your pride get in the way. The Great King is going to call you to a leadership role with His people. But never put the people before your wife. She comes first. Do you understand everything I have told you?"

"Yes, sir," I replied.

"Very good," he said. "We will help you. Besides myself, I give you Nathan as a mentor. Follow his example. Look at how he loves and leads his family, and do likewise. The Great King will soon give you children, and you must train for that as well."

Nathan and I looked at each other and smiled. He was a dear brother to me and a faithful friend.

We suddenly heard a voice behind us. It was Captain Enoch.

"Praise the Great King!" he said as he came and sat with us. "I just heard the great news. What a splendid match!"

"Welcome back," Captain Samuel said to his dear friend. "How were your travels?"

"Very successful," he said. "There is no doubt that the Great King is at work. In nearly every village I visit, there are pockets of people, just like us, trying to stay true to the Scroll. They are not accepting the popular religion of these times, which attempts to mingle the Scroll and the world. I just returned from Greystone, and there is a precious group of beloved brethren there."

"Greystone?" I said in surprise. "I lived there for many years and never saw a group like ours."

"You usually won't see them unless you are looking for them," Captain Enoch replied. "I know for certain, Caleb, that you did see them. You saved their lives. Remember the woman with the children whose lives you and the blacksmith, William, saved?"

"Of course," I replied.

"They are forever in your debt. And they are also true followers of the Great King."

"Really?" I said. "How wonderful! Where do they meet?"

"In an old barn," he replied. "It is down by the river on the southern reaches of the village. About fifty of them gather there often to train."

193

I knew that barn well, for I would often walk down aside the river in my free time. I could remember hearing the sounds of swords clanging and arrows hitting their mark. All that time, only a few hundred yards away from my home in Greystone, was a band of true warriors. I wondered what my life with William would had been like if we had found them and joined them, but in the end, I knew that the plans of the Great King were best.

"When do you think our clans will need to gather as one?" Nathan asked, going back to the initial inquiry of Captain Enoch's quest.

"I can't say," Captain Enoch replied. "The timing of all of this is beyond my vision. But I am certain that it will be obvious. Something will require it to happen. Until then, we must continue to train and be on the lookout."

Captain Samuel denied me the opportunity to say goodnight to my woman, for he said that while betrothed, distance was good. We did see each other, however, from across the fire as I was bid to return home. Our eyes met, and the communication we shared in just that simple glance was profound. I was so thankful for her and the grace that the Great King had given us. I walked home, and although I was excited about my betrothment and the days ahead, I quickly fell asleep.

I woke up early in the morning and got ready for the day. I sat on my front porch, Scroll in hand, and waited for Justin and those with him to arrive. I opened the Scroll and read a random passage. It read:

Teach us to number our remaining days of battle.

I thought of how in only a few days, I would be a husband. I sat and reflected on all that had happened that year. I had gone from being an orphan in a foreign village, to being a member of the Castle, to being a rebel in the forest, to rescuing my long-lost soulmate from dragons. With a past like that, I couldn't even wonder what the future had in store. But I knew that it didn't matter. Whatever came, I would be ready because I had the Scroll. I had the Spirit of the Great King. I had brothers and sisters who lived according to the Scroll. And I had a woman who was incredible.

I then saw Justin coming, and he wasn't alone. Nearly fifty others came with him, men, women, and children. I stood and welcomed them.

"I'm glad to see you," I said to Justin, shaking his hand.

"And I you," he replied. He still didn't look well, as if he had been up all night, troubled and unsure of the truth. Captain Samuel then arrived.

"My friends," he said. "Gather around and listen to my words. You are here because you are concerned with what is happening in the Castle, correct?"

Many nodded in agreement and he continued. "The truth is this: those in the Castle, by and large, have good intentions. Yet much of what they do isn't found in the Scroll but is instead tradition—tradition that has been greatly molded and influenced by the fallen culture of this world. Many of you have been brought up thinking that to enter into that building and to do the things you do when you gather is what the Great King requires of you.

"Listen to me carefully, my friends. Much of what is done in the Castle every King's Day is good, but it is far from the desires of the Great King; indeed, it is overshadowed by much wrongdoing and worldliness. The Great King cares very little about songs and prayers and messages if they don't reflect a life of victory and love. He wants the men in His army to be servant-leaders of their families, to lead their children and love their wives. He wants the women in His army to be helpmeets and homemakers who support and complete their husbands. He wants the parents to train and raise up their children, not for parents to delegate their children to the local magistrate or the Castle but to be the captains of their children. And He wants children to obey and honor their parents, as they quickly grow into men and women of maturity and responsibility.

"The Castle hasn't trained you on how to do this. Indeed, their very way of doing things goes against it and sets you up for defeat. We can train you on how to be the families that the Great King desires for you to be. Not only that, but the Great King desires you to kill dragons, with the men wielding the sword and the women wielding the bow. We can train you on how to do this as well. We don't just talk about victory; we take hold of it.

"But this is what it will require of you: you must train daily, either in your home or with us, and you must put aside all that the world holds dear. Simply put, you must make the Great King, your family, and dragon slaying, your life. These three things are all that remain—the Great King, your families, and killing dragons. If you aren't willing to focus on these things, then you may now go in peace. But if you are willing to daily devote yourself to the priorities of the Great King, then follow me. I know you have questions; they will be answered. But this is the line you must cross. It must be complete devotion or nothing at all."

With that, Captain Samuel turned and headed for the forest. I walked beside him. After only a few yards, I began to turn to see who was following us but he stopped me.

"Do not look," he said. "Wait until we get there. You will gain nothing by looking. If they don't follow now then that is their choice. We must respect it."

I obeyed him and we continued on. I wanted so badly to turn around, for I hoped that all fifty remained. Most of all, I wanted to see if Justin was on board. The anticipation and suspense were extreme. A part of me expected to turn and see no one; another part of me expected to see everyone. We finally made it to the edge of the forest. Captain Samuel and I ceased walking and turned. Only fifteen people remained, and Justin was amongst them. He was smiling, and it seemed a weight had been lifted from him.

"Fifteen of you," Captain Samuel counted. "Very good. That's more than I had expected. Follow me."

He entered the forest. The fifteen followers hesitated and looked at me with fear in their eyes.

"Don't be afraid," I said. "Our meeting place is nearby, and no dragon will come upon us."

They all followed but with hesitation. Justin and I walked together.

"I never thought I would be entering the forest like this," he said. "Am I a rebel now?"

"I suppose that depends on your perspective," I replied. "But according to the Scroll's perspective, you are not a rebel but a son. You are a member of the army of the Great King."

"I'm a little nervous," he said. "My life with the Castle has always been, well, comfortable. I fear that this won't be."

"You're correct," I replied. "It won't be comfortable, but it will be good. Didn't the Great King say that His path was difficult? Didn't He say that only a few find it?"

"Yes, He did," Justin agreed. "Very well. Let the true journey begin."

"Yes!" I said. "The training will begin today, for urgency is always needed."

We entered into the Oasis to the sight of everyone training, the ladies with their bows and the men with their swords. The fifteen new pilgrims were amazed.

"This make so much sense!" Justin said, looking around at the warriors training. "I don't understand how I never thought of this before."

"You were deceived," I said. "And by definition, when you are deceived, you don't know it. So, when the veil is lifted, it is a shock. But don't worry, brother. Just be thankful that the veil is lifted, or better said, is being lifted."

Captain Samuel called everyone together and presented our new recruits.

"These people have counted the cost and have crossed the line. Welcome them. We will train together now, and in doing so, work up an appetite fit for a feast!"

We all welcomed our new brethren with love and kindness. They were all excited and taken aback at what they beheld. I introduced Justin and Elizabeth and told him of our plans to marry.

"You don't waste any time!" he said joyfully.

"Not when I have such an amazing treasure before me," I replied.

Elizabeth bowed with a smile, and along with the other sisters, took the ladies to the archery range while the men gathered around Captain Samuel and Captain Enoch.

"Take your swords in your hands, men," Captain Samuel began. All of the men obeyed.

"Now close your eyes," Captain Enoch ordered. The men obeyed.

The new recruits were scattered from each other, their swords up and eyes closed, while the other men instructed them. Nathan was training Justin. He motioned for me to join him, and together, Nathan and I circled around Justin as we taught him.

"Your sword is not just a sword," Nathan said as he tapped his own sword against Justin's. "It is an extension of the Scroll."

"If your faith and knowledge regarding the Scroll is dull," I added, "then your sword will also be dull. Do you understand?"

"Yes," Justin answered.

I marveled at what was happening. There I was, training a man in the same way I had been trained. This is what the Great King had spoken of in the Scroll when He said, *Go and train soldiers who will train soldiers.*

"Open your eyes," Nathan commanded. Justin obeyed. "In order to fight dragons, you must first get comfortable using your sword," he explained. "I will swing my sword down upon you, and you will block. Don't worry; I won't swing too hard. Then you will turn to Caleb, and he will do the same. Then you will begin to counter our attacks. Are you ready?"

Justin nodded and the training ensued. This went on for half an hour. All the other men were doing likewise, and the Oasis was filled with the pleasant sound of swords clanging. I looked over at Elizabeth from time to time as she helped the new ladies with their form and accuracy. I also witnessed her showing a young lady a more modest and effective way to pull back her hair. Already, in less than an hour, the culture of these recruits was changing. I then understood why Captain Samuel had always been so slow to bring others into our army. Until they are truly ready, and truly convinced, and absolutely all in, training will be slow and hard. But once their hearts are resolute, they quickly progress in proficiency.

"One last time," I said to Justin. "Then we will take a break. This time, when you turn to me, I will swing down upon you twice, then you must counter twice. Don't worry; you won't hurt me. Are you ready? And remember, your sword is an extension of the Scroll. You love the Scroll, Justin. Be courageous. Be bold."

I came down upon him, and he blocked with more courage and confidence than before. Then when he swung upon me, I dodged the first and blocked the second. We looked upon each other, weary from training. Justin's face beamed with joy and satisfaction.

"You are wielding the sword," I said to him with a smile. He smiled back.

"I know," he said. He then looked around at everyone training. "It's what I always wanted. It's perfect and true and wonderful."

Captain Samuel now gathered everyone around for a prayer before the meal.

"You all trained very well," he said. "We will now feast together. But first, I want to invite our dear Caleb to say a few words. He, not long ago, was in many of your shoes."

This took me off guard, but I understood why he did it. In the years to come, according to the prophecy, I would be a leader to these people. He was giving me a step in that direction.

"I know you have many questions," I said to the group. "In time, by the grace of the Great King, they will be answered. For now, be certain of this: This is just the beginning. There is so much more to discover and understand. As long as we stay true to the Scroll, and to each other, we will never fail. The Great King fights for us.

His only terms are that we walk in obedience to His word, which we will gladly do, regardless of the cost. The world will hate you, and the religious may mock you, but the Great King will love you. We will never stop. We will never quit."

Everyone shouted with jubilation. But then, one lone voice came forth from the crowd. It was Justin.

"I am with you," he said plainly. "I will train with you, and I will fight with you, and I will lay down my life for any of you. I am all in. There is only one over-arching issue that remains in my mind."

"And what is that, my son?" Captain Samuel asked.

"Well," he said, looking around at all of us, "here we are training, doing life together, and learning not just what to do but how to actually do it. We are going to slay dragons. We are like-minded. We are a united army under the leadership of the Great King. But alas—and this is my question—where is our Castle? The other people in the village have a Castle, and the Great King said that He is going to build His Castle, so where is our Castle?"

Captain Samuel smiled and slowly turned to me.

"Caleb?" he said.

"Where is our Castle?" I repeated with a smile. "Look around you, my friend. We are the Castle! The Great King never intended for the Castles to be made of actual stone and mortar. His followers, the warriors of His Kingdom, together with one mind are His Castle. He is building us, and He will build us strong."

Epilogue

We crept up to edge of the forest and peered out into the sun-lit prairie. Our number was seven. Captain Samuel was there, as was Nathan and his son Levi, now twenty-three years old. Jedidiah was with us, as well as my dear brother, Justin. And lastly myself and my son, Benjamin, who was nearly seventeen.

It had been more than eighteen years since Justin and those with him joined our cause, and yet in some ways, it felt like only a little while. Benjamin put his hand on my shoulder, and I nodded to him that all was well. The sight we beheld was unnerving.

The Castle glistened in the sunlight, the new marble siding sparkling as a rare jewel. The members of the Castle filed into the building, as they did every King's Day. What drew our attention, however, weren't the people but the two dragons, perched on top of the edifice.

"Those dragons are unleashed," Nathan said.

"It's just as Captain Enoch prophesied," Jedidiah said. "On his death bed, he told us that this would happen."

Captain Samuel stayed quiet as he looked with unwavering resolve and conviction.

"What does this mean?" Benjamin asked quietly.

"It means things are changing," Captain Samuel answered, his aged form standing strong like an oak. "The gentle cough, so to speak, that we witnessed so many years ago has now began a full-blown virus. They allowed the enemy to come into their ranks through compromise and tolerance. And now, they have been consumed. The Castle and the dragons are now one."

"Some of us must get in there," I said. "We must hear the message."

"They will never let any of us in there," Justin said. "You know that."

"There are ways," I said. "We can go in disguise."

"You may get in," Captain Samuel answered. "But I can save you the trouble. Their message is simple. The dragons are no longer the enemies but are now the allies. They are one. The dragons will convince them of a new enemy, an enemy that is intolerant and uncompromising."

"You mean us?" Nathan asked.

"There's no doubt about it," Captain Samuel said. "We will still hunt dragons, but now the Castles of this world will be hunting us."

The adventure continues in:

The Dragon and the King & The Maiden and the Serpent

The Castle and the Scroll and the Dragon and the King are also available as audio books.

CHRISTIANITY AND GOVERNMENT
The education that brings freedom

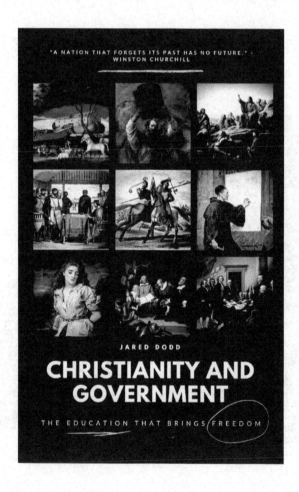

The DIO Trilogy
Discipleship Series

Discipleship 10-week video study

(Streamable & downloadable)

Discipleship Book & Kindle editions

Discipleship MP3 audio

Discipleship DVD set

Immersion 10-week video study

(Streamable & downloadable)

Immersion Book & Kindle editions

Immersion MP3 audio

Obedience 20-week video study

(Streamable & downloadable)

Obedience Book & Kindle editions

Obedience MP3 audio

PRIEST & WARRIOR
The Tale of Benaiah

The nation of Israel is being torn apart from both within and without. King Saul has been rejected and rumors grow that a young shepherd boy has been anointed to take his place. Benaiah is a young priest who only desires to serve his king. But as tensions rise Benaiah is faced with a difficult choice: Will he remain with Saul, or will he become an outlaw by joining with David?

THE ESSENTIALS
16 qualities that will set your child up for success

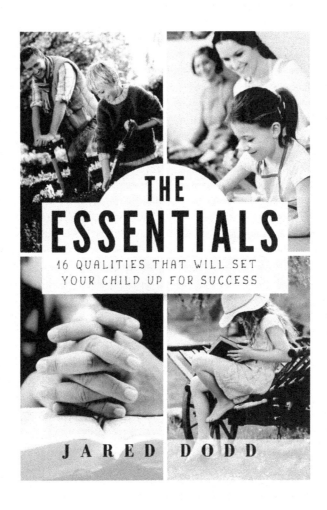

Made in USA - North Chelmsford, MA
1309305_9781790830725
03.23.2022 1006